Temptation In Black

Blackstone, Volume 2

Rachel E Rice

Published by Rachel E Rice, 2024.

Temptation in Black
Book 2 Blackstone Series
Copyright 2013 by Rachel E. Rice
Re-edited in 2022

Author's Note:

You can contact me at rachelerice04@gmail.com or visit my website/blog: http://www.rachel-e-rice.com

Table of Contents

Prologue

Alex read the yearning in Max's handsome face, which was awash with dangerous contradictions. His smoldering eyes sent electrical waves caressing her body. She felt the heat rise from within and settle deep in her clit. He needed her mouth. He needed to disappear into Alex. He needed to disappear into her body. Her mouth was the conduit where all his tension flowed, but until she found out the truth about the dead girl, she had to keep him calm, and the best way she knew was to give him the pleasure he craved.

Alex's lush eyelashes lifted. She gazed on Max's open shirt, which revealed his hard, rippling abs. Her hand caressed each one. He was her guilty pleasure—her temptation in black.

She reached and held Max's hard penis in her hands, and a smile crept across his face. His thumb slid over her lips. Knowing how his body would react, she teased it by circling the head of his shaft around her open mouth. Blowing soft, warm air, she watched Max's eyes flutter and close. With a slight parting of his lips, a wisp of air shuttled out. "Yes, yes, you know what to do to me," he whispered. Her hand moved the length of his hard cock, up and down.

Alex opened her mouth wide. Guiding his penis in slowly, she sucked it, harder. His eyes remained shut. He was in a world of his own—blissful sexual peace. He mumbled something low, and Alex couldn't hear his words clearly. She thought he whispered, "I love you, I love you... Rebecca," or was it Alex? She felt his arousal; his penis was increasing in her mouth, growing longer and wider. He pushed his hips into her, and she reached for him and sank her hands into his hard ass. She felt it flex and tighten. Leaning her face over him, she felt as if she couldn't take another inch, when to her surprise, the muscles in her throat relaxed.

With her hands massaging his buttocks and her mouth clamped firmly around his penis, Alex sucked harder, driving him into a world of pleasure and heights of ecstasy. She was taking everything from him, and try as he might, he couldn't resist her. She had taken control of his sexual life and without her, what would he do? No woman had ever satisfied him as completely as Alex.

The thought of having another woman besides Alex—he refused to entertain the idea.

Alex tasted a hint of warm come on her tongue, and she knew that he was over the edge. She was controlling this man who was used to being in charge. She was now the puppet master, and it felt great with a man like him—a handsome sexual animal.

Drawing her mouth in with one hard suck, his body contorted, then Max let out a primal sound of erotic ecstasy, and his eyes opened like the shutter of a camera. His gaze locked on her. Warm fluid flowed into Alex's mouth. He breathed in and out. His chest moved up and down. She met his gaze, then closed her eyes, and with a slight raise of her head, she swallowed his come.

It was a challenging gesture, and he knew it. He was aware that she was in control.

Alex's eyes opened, holding his glance. Her body was excited from the pleasure she had given Max. With eyes wide and his breathing heavy, Max said, "Damn, Alex, you took my orgasm from me when I wasn't ready. This has never happened to me before." A mischievous grin escaped from Alex—eyes sparkling with warmth and achievement, enjoying her power.

She thought, *There is always the first time for everything, my dangerous, handsome Mr. Black.*

Chapter 1

"Why did you do that, Alex? You knew I wasn't ready. What's wrong with you?" He glanced down at her. "Are you becoming dangerous to me?" Max's voice heightened with cool restraint, which caused the hair on Alex's arm to rise. He sounded like a wounded animal. *How could something be wrong, you handsome, crazy fuck? I just read that your fiancée has been found strangled, and you didn't tell me about your twin brother. How could anything be wrong? I'm not the one lying around one of your apartments dead. I'm perfectly happy.*

Voicing her thoughts was not an option, since she was riding in his limo with darkened windows, and Max still had an erection, and the doors were locked. His bodyguard/driver, a burly Asian named Shu, who resembled a ninja warrior dressed in black, never as much as spoke or smiled at her. With an out-of-control sex addict and a ninja warrior, there wasn't much she could do or say.

Concentrating was also out of the question. Her heart beat so loud that she thought she was being strangled by her own fears. The newspaper's headline screamed in her head: **Fiancée of Maximilian Blackstone: Strangled.**

"Nothing is wrong, Max. Why do you ask?" she murmured, glancing up into his to-die-for face from her kneeling position. She forced a wide smile. *I'm in the right position for praying. Praying that my judgment isn't as flawed as I think, and that I didn't select a murderer to father my child. I guess I am nothing but a desperate, eligible, eager, foolish young woman.*

Max leaned in Alex's direction and extended his hand to caress her hair. She flinched. He saw her movement, but nothing registered.

"You've changed," he said, threading his fingers through her hair, hoping to coax her to complete what he'd started—fucking her, or at least letting him come while eating her out. She knew he needed all this so he could get a good night's sleep. "One minute you are raising my blood pressure with that beautiful mouth of yours, and the next minute it is as if your heart has stopped beating for me. Normally you're wet and breathing hard when I insert my fingers into that pretty little cunt."

"Can you stop talking to me like that?" Alex demanded.

Max's eyes darkened, his brow furrowed, and his lips were taut.

"Are you planning on telling me what is wrong with you, and why you are behaving like a child, or do you expect me to read your mind?" Max said, impatient and agitated. His stare was long and focused. She couldn't connect the warmth of his green eyes with the coldness in his voice, or a woman strangled in an apartment.

"I'm feeling cold, because I can't get out of my mind that you would allow your twin brother to fuck me." Alex's voice, full of anger and confusion, rang throughout the car. She raised her body from a kneeing position.

She sat beside Max, gazing coldly into his eyes, never losing her focus.

"So, you're leaving me crazy with wanting your body," he said, fixated on Alex's plump lips. "You know I have this problem with sleep."

Take some Excedrin PM, you sexy, horny fuck.

"Do you have another man? Maybe it's my brother that you want, Alex?"

"I'm not going to answer that, because it's madness on your part."

"You know I need you more than you can imagine." Zipping his pants, he pulled Alex's black lace thong from his pocket. It had fallen from the white robe that covered her naked body. "I suppose you will need this," he said, inhaling the crotch of her thong with his eyes closed. Alex reached for it, but he put it behind his back and then suspended it on his finger in front of her.

"I can never get enough of your smell. It's fresh and reminds me of the ocean. If you don't satisfy me soon… I don't know what I will do next." That statement captured Alex's attention; she kicked the newspaper farther under the seat and out of sight. She lowered her head, and her eyes wandered.

What more do you want, you sex addict? Alex focused.

Snatching the thong from his finger, she gave a small huff and then put it back in the pocket of the robe. It barely concealed anything. Now she wanted to hide her disgust with Max, and her shame for falling for a man that she had gone to any lengths to get and keep.

Raising her head and eyes, she said, "You never explain anything, Max. Why did you send me to that place, never telling me that he was your brother?"

"For God's sake, Alex, must we go through this again? I explained to you that I didn't know that you were Rebecca," he stated with a raised eyebrow, which made him more attractive to Alex, if that were possible. That dangerous perturbed look on his face only made Alex's clit vibrate, and she felt the heat settle inside her. She wanted to take him home and suck his dick until he begged her to stop. She wanted to drain him of all his come until he had nothing left for another woman, because if she walked away from him, he would have someone waiting to take her place.

Alex needed an explanation, even if it was a lie.

She needed to sleep at night without worrying that she would be his next victim. She didn't know how to separate herself from the man she lived for, but didn't want to die for.

"And that's how you treat women you bring into your world? You pass them off to your brother to be fucked."

Max's eyes darkened as he remembered. "I was explicit, No intercourse, and especially not anal intercourse." His eyes met hers. "You must have done something for him to make him want you in that manner. You're not exactly his type."

Alex's eyes burned into Max. "What type is that? Maybe it's because I'm a woman, and I was naked. Did that occur to you?" Alex's brow furrowed, her eyes narrowed, and she glared with anger. "You could have warned Rebecca, but you were hot for me, after all I did to satisfy your sick hunger." *Oh, this is crazy. What I'm saying is absolutely insane. It was my choice to pretend to be Rebecca.*

Closing her eyes, Alex placed her hands on both sides of her head and leaned back.

"What you did for me was drive me to my limits with that beautiful body and dirty phone sex. You never let me know the real you. It was your responsibility to reveal your identity and notify me that I have a son, but you didn't. You disappeared and I could never find you," Max said, reaching for her hands and pulling them and placing them in her lap.

"You were too busy tying up women and concentrating on your erotic pleasures to look for me. How many did you have to use that tongue and finger on, and those anal beads before you found the right woman to fit your dick?"

Max raised his index finger and pointed. "Only one. You." His gaze shrouded Alex. "You were so busy with your anger and revenge, and enjoying me whipping your ass that..."

Alex shouted, "I've had enough. Let me out now! I can walk home." *Who the fuck is he to tell me that I enjoy him spanking my ass, when it is his fault that I am fucked up like this? I've never even fathomed doing anything as profound as allowing a man to place anal beads in my ass, let alone fucking a man that wants to be led around with a collar. I didn't get that screwed up until I laid eyes on his freaky ass,* Alex thought.

"You're behaving like a child."

"I am a child compared to you. What are you, thirty or forty?"

He paused to look into Alex's eyes, and a sly grin slid across his mouth. "I'm thirty-three, and everyone your age thinks thirty-three is old, but I'm the right age for you and the right man for you, my darling."

He leaned to kiss Alex, but she moved quickly, changing to a seat across from him to get away from his natural sexual heat, the kind of heat a woman could lose herself in with the smell of sex. He had a body to die for, and she knew that she would die if he replaced her. The only woman she knew about was the one lying in a delicate position, a position she hoped would not happen to her, because she had to get away from him until she uncovered the truth.

"I'm not about to allow you to run around San Francisco naked with just a robe covering that pretty body. It makes me hot thinking about you." Alex's eyes narrowed and she bristled. Max reached and touched his penis. "See what you've done to me. I can't see you or think about you without a hard-on. Do you know what you've done? I can't let you go. I can't allow another man to have you," he stated with a dangerous, dark tone. *There is that word again—allow.* His eyes peered at her from behind his lush black eyelashes.

"Is everything about you fucking and satisfying your needs?"

"You are the only woman that has this effect on my body. What do you want me to do? Do you want me to look for another woman? Is that what you want? Are you sending me out into that world that I just escaped from?" *What am I to tell him? Yes, go on out there and find someone, and see if I can stand you lusting and making love to another woman while I go crazy. The way I want you, Mr. Black, I could resort to torture. Let's see. I would take you to a secret place, make you strip, put a collar around your neck, tie you up, and suck you and never let you come, and if you just happened to, I would whip you until your ass was sore.*

What is wrong with me? I have lost my mind. You see what you have done to me, Mr. Black? I'm here contemplating torture. Well, there is nothing wrong with thinking; it's only wrong when we act out our dangerous fantasies.

Alex lowered her sight to his hard body. She watched his body vibrate and his breath quicken. She had never seen him so sexually aroused. She wanted his warm come to flow into her body so that he would not have any left to fill another woman.

When Max calmed, he spoke softly. "I'll take you home. I have wasted too much time..."

"Fine. Now I'm a waste of time." Alex crossed her arms in a huff, and sat back in the seat as they rode the remaining mile to the apartment in silence. Max met and held Alex's gaze. She felt uncomfortable, because she couldn't get out of her mind the headlines in the newspaper. *Clearly he will never explain anything to me. He never does*, she thought. *What's the use asking again?*

"Alex, why are you editing my words to use against me? Do you need another orgasm? I can give you one before you leave," Max said, tilting his head to the right with a haughty, arrogant smirk.

"You are impossible, Max." Alex bit her lip to keep from screaming, and she shot him the finger. The limo came to a stop in front of Blackstone's luxurious apartment building. Alex reached to open the door, pulling feverishly at the handle.

"You're not leaving here angry."

"And what are you going to do about it?"

"Placing you over my knee and spanking you is not good enough." He smiled softly, trying to soothe Alex's anger. "I could take you back to my hotel and fuck you and give you something that you have never had," he said with a threatening sneer and a curl of his lips.

"Now you're resorting to kidnapping and fucking me while choking me." Max's eyes grew large and dark. His brow furrowed, and he raised one eyebrow. A smile never left his lips. His jaws tightened. *What does Alex know about sexual asphyxiation?* Max thought.

"If I fucked you while choking you, you would enjoy every minute of it. I don't just fuck you, I make love to you."

What the fuck did I say, and what the fuck am I hearing? Alex caught herself, because she hadn't plan on confronting Max this way; it just slipped out.

"You know better, Alex. I would never hold you against your will," Max addressed one of Alex's concerns.

I know, you beautiful, seductive man. I just can't resist you. This is not normal. Nothing about Mr. Black is normal. How could I think that I could ever have a life with him? This is a serious mental health issue, and I need help, but he *needs it more*, she thought.

Once Max's words could have showered her with wanton desire and she would be on her knees, but now she wasn't sure about him. Not even about his brother. He should have told her about Jonas, that handsome freak who'd had her hot and ready to let him tie her up.

"What is wrong with you, Alex?" Max said in a quiet and measured voice. "Is it your time of the month... your period? Am I using the correct terminology?"

Alex rolled her eyes upward, and they closed for a second. "Don't provide an excuse. For heaven's sake let me out of here."

Max unlocked the door, and his driver got out and held the door open for Alex.

After stepping out of the limo, Alex leaned in as Max's long legs extended out.

"Don't see me into the apartment." Alex felt her ploy didn't work. She couldn't goad him into confessing. He was always in control of what he said, but when it came to sex with her, she knew he was out of control. Maybe she should wait until she had him wanting her and then she would ask him that pertinent question.

"What can I do for you, Alex?"

"I want you to give me time to forget all of this, and for you to clean up the mess in your life."

"And what about my son? Am I to get more time with Maxim? He's two, and I've missed the most important time in his life."

"He has been my son longer than he has been yours. I'll decide when you can see him."

"Oh, Alex, that's not fair." She'd found his soft spot, his weakness, and she was satisfied for the moment. She knew that Max could be ruthless. After all, he was Maximilian Blackstone, and you didn't get that rich without leaving bodies on the floor.

Max watched Alex step out of the car. His face wore a sullen and distraught look. Maybe Alex wasn't being fair, maybe she should discuss the murder of the young woman and not jump to conclusions, but clearly she had given Max every opportunity to say something, anything that would mitigate the doubts that coursed through her mind. With her head lowered, she scurried into her apartment to call Joshua.

"Joshua, can you come over? I'm feeling a little crazy now."

"What's the matter now, Alex? That maniac has you twisted in his trap?"

"Just come up now, and if you have some ice cream bring that too."

"This sounds serious." Joshua hung up and Alex dashed into the shower, threw on a pink exercise pant suit, and opened the elevator door.

"Come in, Joshua." Joshua stood at the entrance, lounging in a black T-shirt and jeans. The tee had bold letters in gold: **Blackstone Hotels: we provide the best food and a good night's sleep.** *Yeah, sure you do, Blackstone. What a load of crap. You can't even get a good night's sleep unless your dick is lodged inside me.*

"Is it safe?" he asked, hesitating, and peeping around. Still standing in the elevator, looking unusually handsome with his windswept hair, Joshua said, "You look kind of strange. I don't know if I want to mix my good karma with yours." She grabbed his wrist and pulled him in and took the French vanilla ice cream into the kitchen. Placing two scoops into each of two crystal bowls, she brought it out to Joshua, handing one bowl to him with a spoon. She sat and peered into the bowl, then, scooping a spoonful into her mouth, her eyes shifted over to Joshua.

He laid the bowl down. "I'm waiting for you to tell me why you look as if you've lost your favorite dog," Joshua said, leaning back in a chair with his legs and arms crossed. Alex sat facing him on the opposite side of the decorative fireplace.

"It's Max."

"Well, in that case you have lost your favorite dog."

Alex rolled her eyes at Joshua. "This is serious, Joshua. Are you going to shut up and listen? Max has a twin brother and he never told me."

"You never told him that you were masquerading as Rebecca the slut."

"Please, Joshua, let's not go down that road; it's a bridge to nowhere. I have more important things to tell you." There was a long pause.

"Well?"

"For one, I have a son, and I think Max is a killer."

"What the fuck, Alex? What the fuck. No way." Joshua jumped up, twisting his head left and right with his eyes closed. He circled the Italian yellow leather chair with his hands tucked into the pockets of his low-rider jeans.

"What? No way he's a murderer?" Alex questioned with a defeated glance.

"No. No way you had a baby and didn't tell me, and yes, I knew that rich cunt was strange. I wouldn't be surprised if a body shows up." Joshua raked his fingers through his hair.

"One already has. Have you read today's paper?"

Joshua took a large mouthful of ice cream. "He may be strange, but he's not a murderer. I would have known. But he is a bit of a thug."

"What are you talking about?"

"Do you hear the way he talks when he's not trying to impress with that refined speech of his? When he wants something he takes it, and when he wanted to know if I had a relationship with you, he walked up to me and asked if I was fucking you. Just like that. Enough said." Alex listened tentatively.

Joshua walked to Alex's wine fridge, took out a bottle of wine, uncorked it, reached for a glass on a rack, and poured himself a large glass of wine. He returned to see Alex in the same position with the bowl empty.

"No one knows anyone that well," Joshua murmured, sitting with his shoulders forward, close to Alex's face. "You don't know anything about him. I had to tell you that he was married three times and divorced and that he had a fiancée all the while he was seeing you, I mean Rebecca. Did he even introduce you to his parents?"

Alex leaned forward with both hands on her legs, and said, "Well, the fiancée is dead. And I thought his mother and father were dead."

Joshua spilled his glass of wine and reached for a napkin, then took a large gulp.

"Who's to say you won't be next or your friends? I told you he was dangerous."

"You said 'trouble,' not 'dangerous.' And there's nothing to suggest that he would go after friends. Don't be so dramatic, Joshua."

Alex's smartphone rang. She quickly placed it to her ear. "Alex, this is Max. I couldn't leave you being angry with me. Can I come to see you tonight? I need you. We never talked about our son and our wedding."

"Max, have you read the papers today?"

"No."

"I did, and I think that you should." Alex heard Max ask for the paper and then there was a long silence. "What do you have to say about that?"

"That does not concern me, Alex. I had nothing to do with that young woman's demise."

"But she was your fiancée."

"I broke it off with her when you came into my life. I was so happy to have you back in my life... let me see you and explain everything."

"Okay, Max, give me a few hours." How could she say no when she hungered for his touch? She wanted to feel his hands move over her skin and travel down the nape of her neck to her buttocks. He liked to place his hand on one cheek at a time as she lay on her stomach, massaging them and making her ready for him. While she lay on her stomach he would insert his long finger into her vagina and then her anus to arouse her and prepare her for his penis. Alex couldn't help but run these images through her mind, and they were making her hot. Her body could not contain the pent-up sexual desires that he ignited.

The image of his handsome face and dark expressions drove her crazy. What he did with his fingers could drive her to unbelievable ecstasy.

"I'll be there by seven."

"Alex, I'm leaving," Joshua whispered.

"Who is that, Alex?" Max said in a demanding voice.

"You don't answer my questions, and I'm not going to answer yours."

His voice weakened. "Why are you being so cruel to me? You know I can't stand you behaving like that. I'm coming over now, and if you have a man in there I am going to be awfully pissed with you." And he hung up the phone.

"Joshua, you have to leave now."

"You can't allow him to control your life," Joshua stated, walking in the direction of the elevator.

"I know. I don't want you to lose your job. And I need to see him; after all, we have a child together."

"Well, since you mentioned my job, I'm going." Joshua opened the door and turned. "Don't forget, Alex—I'm close. If you need me, call and I'll be there in a quick second. Keep your phone near."

"Yeah... yeah, Joshua. I'll be okay." Alex pushed Joshua into the elevator and closed the door.

Alex rushed to comb her hair. She put it in a ponytail and pulled it up on top of her head. Her bangs covered her forehead, which she thought was far too large, but Max said that he liked it. Strands fell on both sides of her face, framing it. She swiped a thin layer of gloss over her lips to make them luscious, just the way Max liked them. *Why am I still trying to please him?* she thought. The answer came back. *I love him. I love that handsome, fuckable man. I love being with him and I love the way he makes love to me.*

But is that a good reason to be with a man? she asked herself. *For now, it is the best reason I can come up with. If I can't see him I think I would die*, she thought.

She heard the elevator, his key in the door, and there he stood, sexy, tall, brimming with sex appeal so much so that he could bottle it and sell it. She could smell his Tom Ford Noir signature scent. He was irresistible. Alex stood in the doorway of the bedroom, leading to the living area. She didn't want to move. Her breath shortened as she just took him in, all of him. His hair and beard were cut short.

That makes him the sexiest man alive, she thought.

He leaned against the wall with one leg crossing the other. His dark pants hugged his small waist, and muscles flexed under his black V-neck silk sweater. She had never seen anyone who could make the color black look so inviting and so sexy.

"Come here, Alex," Max said darkly, waving his right hand back and forth and gesturing for her to come to him. "If you don't come to me, I'll have to walk over there, and then I'm going to take you to bed and spank you, maybe tie you up." His eyes lowered. "If you don't want me to take you, then come here." Max's voice rang dark and deep.

Standing holding on to the frame of the door, she locked her gaze on Max. His unbelievable sexy jade eyes seduced her once again. His face, covered lightly with a manicured beard, appeared different, as if he was another man. It was as if she was seeing him for the first time, and he looked delicious, and she couldn't move, because she wanted what he had been giving her—unbelievable orgasms.

Come and take every part of me, you handsome, sexy fuck. I want you so much that I don't care what you have done before. I just need you now. I need to take your dick in my mouth and let your come flow down my lips and on my nipples. I want to smear your life all over my body, you handsome, dangerous fuck.

Max read that look on her face because he had seen it many times with Rebecca, but she no longer wore the blonde wig to fool him. There was no need, because he wanted his Alex, and he had his Rebecca. He got both, and now it was time to find out how it felt to have his virgin and his slut.

He sauntered over to her on his long legs, and when he reached her he wrapped his arms around her and pulled her violently to him. Looking at her, he said, "I've wanted to treat Alex rough and with no holds barred, but I was afraid. I thought that you would hate me, and that's why I continued my relationship with Rebecca. Don't you see I need this, and you like the way I make love to you in bed?"

Max cupped her mouth with his lips and slashed through it, hungry for her tongue. He sucked her tongue as he pulled her top open, and each snap came undone one by one. Then he pulled her pants down and found she had nothing on beneath. His eyes burned as he scanned her protruding nipples. A smile escaped.

Alex's mouth moved slowly from Max's lips. She helped him raise his sweater over his head. She could feel his muscles flex hard as they brushed her skin. She reached down and unbuttoned his pants, and they dropped. As Max stepped out of them, his body was bare and his hard dick stood strong, pressing against Alex's bald mound.

Placing his fingers between her legs, he found the folds surrounding her tense clit. Touching it softly, his fingers circled it, and then he dropped his head down to her breasts and stuck his index finger into her vagina. He pushed it in, then pulled it out, and said, "You are ready for me. You are so wet and sweet."

He slammed her against the wall with his mouth sucking her breasts; he rammed his dick into her with a powerful growl. "Yes, Alex, you know what I like." Alex pushed her mound into him, grinding up and down, left, and right. Her vaginal muscles caressed and stroked his penis. His voice weak, he said, "You are so good, Alex. That clit is so sweet. I don't know what I would do if you ever left me."

She leaned her body into his, and he pinned her against the wall. He lifted her, and she wrapped her legs around his waist. "Yes… yes, give it to me the way I like."

"What do you want, Max?"

"You know." Alex moved away from Max's impossibly hard dick. He rolled her around, and she slid down and began sucking him. He leaned against the wall, his head back, his mouth open, his legs spread, with Alex on her knees with his hard dick firmly in her mouth.

"Oh, Alex, when did you get so good? I would do something horrible if I thought I couldn't have you this way." He pushed and pulled his penis in and out of her mouth as Alex held it with a suction that drove him wild. After all, it was him who had taught her how to please him and now it was out of his control. He pulled out, because he was wound so tight that he would have spilled his come in her mouth. Max was still shy around Alex, even though he had engaged in BDSM with her. He wanted to experience it again, but he didn't want to rush it.

Going to his knees, he placed Alex on her back on the floor, and then, leaning over her, he kissed her neck and trailed his tongue down between her breasts and past her navel, and he bit her thighs. He glanced up at Alex and laid his head between her legs. He hoisted her legs onto his shoulders, and softly licked her folds and clit. Her clit throbbed, and he knew she was ready to burst. He would control how she had her orgasm. He always controlled that part of her body, and he would do so now.

It was the sound of her moaning, calling out, "Max... Max," that turned him on and made him weak for her. He would do anything for Alex to keep her. He licked her clit and took her to the point of orgasm and then stopped. "Max, I love you. I love you."

That was all Max wanted to hear, then he sucked her until he felt the quiver of her bud. She was ready, and then like clockwork, his tongue touched lightly under her clit, and she screamed with pleasure.

"I want you Max; give me your dick. I want it now."

Max lay across Alex and his penis found her heated vagina. It seared him and pleasured him, and the minute his penis touched the fullness of her walls, he oozed come until he passed out over Alex.

They sprawled on the rug, and she lay in his arms. Alex looked over and saw that he was asleep. She stood up, walked, and took a satin blanket from the linen closet and placed over him. Alex shook Max and tried to wake him, but she couldn't. Tired, she found the bed and fell across it.

When her alarm went off, she woke, hopped out of bed, and rushed into the living room where she had left Max. He was gone. *He could have said something*, she thought. *How are we going to solve our problems if all he does is fuck and disappear? What kind of life will I have with this man?*

Alex dressed for work. After all, she hadn't married Max, and she hadn't quit her job. She wanted to speak with Max, and maybe she could at his main office. If she got there early enough, then she might have a chance.

She headed out of her apartment into the lobby.

"Ms. Johns." She turned. It was the doorman. "Someone by the name of Mr. Shu delivered your Mercedes. It's in the garage. Do you want me to have it brought up?"

"No, I'm walking this morning." Alex needed time to think. Walking helped her when her mind was cloudy and mixed up. She hadn't solved anything with Max. It occurred to her that there wasn't enough walking time to wade through her problems, because she stood looking up at the words blackstone written in front of the building. "I'm here already?"

Max's limo wasn't anywhere, but he had several cars, and he could have driven any one of the expensive cars parked outside with a chauffeur waiting. And then she remembered that the blue Rolls Royce was his. The windows were dark. He liked his cars dark, because that was where he found the time to fuck, she imagined. *He could be fucking in it now as I'm standing outside*, she thought.

Because she was early, she saw only the guards stationed at their desk. They smiled, and she entered the elevator. Stopping on the twenty-sixth floor, she saw a light on as she stepped out of the elevator. He was in. Her breathing deepened as she headed for her office. Opening the door, she thought it strange that she hadn't seen Ms. Corday, who managed to be there by 7 a.m. each morning. Alex wondered how she did that, and still looked so perfect each morning with her makeup in perfect order, not a strand of hair out of place. She reminded Alex of a mannequin. She had the same smile day after day.

Alex, on the other hand, could barely make it into work by nine. On some days she didn't show and worked from home.

Walking in, she dropped her purse in the nearest drawer, and scurried to the door to Max's adjoining office. She wanted to have a civilized discussion without sex. Quietly, she opened the door; she wanted to surprise him. She still had her stilettos and handcuffs in her desk. Maybe she would give him a taste of Rebecca if their conversation went well.

"Max!" she shouted. He craned his neck and glanced around at the sound of someone calling. He was naked and on all fours, and Ms. Corday was seated on the leather couch, dressed in a leather corset, her hairless mound visible, with his face planted between her legs. Her high-heeled black thigh-high boots rested on his shoulders. His butt was bruised from the leather strap, and he had Alex's studded collar around his neck.

Chapter 2

"Come back, Alex. It's not what you think," he shouted, his green eyes wide with surprise, his head angled to the right, and his hands outstretched apologetically.

Turning on her heels, Alex rushed into her office and slammed the door with a boom. Her heart was beating loudly, and she checked her pulse, because she thought she would faint. She fumbled around, looking for her purse, her mind blank. She couldn't remember where she'd put it. *Not on the back of the chair*, she thought. Maybe she'd left it in Max's office. *No. No. No*, she reasoned. Finally, her brain began to work, and she grabbed her purse from her desk drawer. She bolted for the elevators.

Hearing a scuffle in Max's office, Alex spun around and peered at his door, but before it could open, the elevator was there in front of her. Turning around, she spied the body of a man standing in the open doorway wearing only his pants. *There is no mistaking that body*, she thought as she dashed in the elevator and the door closed behind her. Alex beat on the button as if it could hasten the speed. She wanted out of there—out of that building and out of his life.

All she could think about was Max with his head in another woman's crotch—his long arms reaching Corday's breasts as his biceps flexed firmly like two rocks, his abdominal muscles bulging, and his small, sexy waist and long legs.

She should have been thinking about the sight of Max parading around naked like a dog, allowing that woman to take her man and her job, but she couldn't think about those things. She would forget the picture in her mind of Max, but she would not forget the feeling he gave her in her heart when she saw him.

Her anger rose moment by moment until she was blind. She could not contain her feelings of betrayal. She had to get relief, or she might do something that was typical—run and hide like a child that couldn't accept painful memories.

Tears welled in her eyes. Alex rushed out of the elevator with her eyes lowered, past her secretary coming in for work, past the guards on the main floor. Through the perfect glass doors, she scampered. The tears flowed down, and her face was drenched. With her head downcast from the sun and from her heartache, covering her red eyes with her hand, she ran to the apartment that had the sign of blackstone in bold letters. Everywhere she turned she saw Blackstone. She was so angry that she picked up a small rock and tossed it at the sign, and when that didn't reach it, she took off one sneaker and hurled it with all her energy. It hit one of the lights, shattering the B and darkening it. Now the sign flashed lackstone. *How can I get him out of my life?* she thought.

The elevator in the apartment seemed slow, and she hammered the button to the penthouse until finally it came. After entering the apartment, she fell in the corner of the foyer, holding her knees to her chest and rocking. Sitting on the cold marble floor, she found no warmth, but it gave her a new perspective on life. She stood and dried her tears with the sleeve of her white shirt and rushed to pack. She would go home to Seattle and see her parents and be with her son, Maxim.

She would leave everything that had to do with Mr. Black—his car, his ring, his sexy body. Yes, the wonderful sex she enjoyed. Just thinking about him tore her apart.

Alex had endured enough; she wanted to be rid of Max. And she would wean herself off of that rich, handsome fuck, who drove her crazy with lust, even if it took years. Then she could lessen his control over her, and she would begin to start her life anew, she and her son. Those were her short-term plans. Long term, she hadn't thought about that, and now would not be the time.

Whenever she thought of her son, Maxim, it was as her son. But he was Max's son too, and it suddenly occurred to her that she would have him in her life forever. Max was a mistake. She could handle mistakes, but could she handle him? How would he take her leaving him? Where would she hide? There weren't enough places in the world that he wouldn't look.

She paused for a few minutes and then walked, snatching her cheap dresses hidden in the back of her closet. She had known she would need them some day. That day had come, and sooner than she had planned. She still sobbed to herself, but she wasn't naïve enough to think that it was all Max's fault.

It was her choice. She didn't have to accept the job, especially since she knew some of the requirements—dirty talk and sex with Blackstone. *I can handle that*, she had thought. The other stuff was far outside of her expertise, yet she managed to learn what it took to keep that rich, beautiful fuck satisfied. "Was it worth it?" she questioned between trails of tears that fell though she continuously wiped them from her eyes. "He was worth every bit of it," she mumbled as tears dripped into her mouth. He had taught her a lesson in life that her parents had said many times. *Everything in life comes with a price, but the question remains: Do you want to pay the price?* "I love him and now he is unfaithful, and I have no one. I don't want anyone but him. What am I to do?"

Some prices are higher than others, she thought.

She gathered the expensive designer dresses in her arms and threw them on the floor. She wanted Max to see the depths of her anger because of his betrayal. She sank in the middle of the Vera Wang gown she had not seen before. She looked at the label, and it said: *To Alex for our wedding day.* Alex pulled the dress to her face then buried herself in it, crying and laughing. *"What the fuck is this Max? Fuck you, Max! Fuck you!"* Alex tore the dress apart piece by piece with her hands, and then she found scissors and began cutting it. She had destroyed a thirty-thousand-dollar dress, her wedding gown, and she felt fine.

Knowing that she wanted his cool, sexy ass and that she wanted him all to herself would command a lot of her time and life. But how did you claim a man like that without risking it all and then losing yourself in the mix? That was her dilemma, and she had no answers. She threw the pieces of the dress aside and stuffed her bag with her old clothes—a few sweaters, wool pants, a black leather jacket and cotton shorts, jeans, and dresses.

Standing and taking one last look, she asked herself, *Where did he expect me to wear this?* She held up a long black gown with the back cut out to the waist. *He never invited me to any of his functions at his hotels or charity events*, she mused.

Her smartphone rang as she tossed her favorite designer dress in the pile.

"Alex, sweetheart, I need you."

"You always need me for your kinky sex. I'm not..."

"Listen for once?" His voice was commanding and dark.

Alex calmed. "I'm listening."

"Will you accompany me to a fundraiser for the protection of the environment?"

"Oh, that is special; the very man who spoils the environment is now protecting it."

"Is that a yes or no?"

"I wouldn't miss it for the world."

"The limousine will pick you up at 7 p.m. Friday. Wear one of the long dresses I selected for you, the black one. You'll know it when you see it, and don't wear any panties."

"What is it, a fundraiser or an orgy?"

"Please, Alex, do as I ask for once."

"If I go with you, I need you to answer some questions. Remember I'm only going with you under certain conditions, and then I'm done."

"What do you mean 'done'? Done with what and whom?"

"I'll answer that when I look into your eyes. We will start with what I saw in your office."

"What did you see?" *He can't be serious. I guess he's going to say I imagined everything.*

"I'm not going to continue this conversation until I see you." And she dropped his call.

———◦———

ALEX HAD A DAY TO PREPARE. She had never been to any social functions with Max. They spent their days and nights hidden away in her penthouse apartment, which he had kept for her and for him to slip in and out when his dick was hard, and that was every day and night.

She called Joshua. "I need your help."

"What? Putting a stake in Blackstone's heart?"

"Be serious. Can you suggest a place where I can get my hair cut and styled?"

"I can probably do it for you along with the psychiatric duties."

"Are we going to act like adults? I have a date with Max for an environmental fundraiser and I need some expert help with my hair and makeup."

"You know that I was invited to his event and all of San Francisco is likely to be there, so I wouldn't put too much stock in his intentions. With that murder hanging over his head, I bet it's a publicity stunt."

"Well, you really know how to rain on a girl's parade."

"When you're caught in a downpour, what's a few more raindrops?" Joshua chuckled. "I think I can help. I'll make you an appointment with a hairstylist I've been seeing on and off."

"Fucking."

"You sound surprised. Or is it jealousy I detect?"

"Neither, Joshua. I knew you wouldn't wait for me forever. You're a great guy."

"I would wait forever, through Blackstone and children if I thought I had a chance with you."

"Don't get so dramatic, Josh." Joshua's emotions spilled out like water from a crack in a dam. He regained his composure, but Alex could hear in his voice the longing and desperation of someone in love, or someone who wanted to be in love. She recognized it, because that was how she felt about Max.

"Go to Blackstone's Omni hotel and ask for Sheila. She'll hook you up."

"Thanks, Josh."

"No problem. I have to go. Some of us have to work for a living."

Alex dressed and drove to the hotel. It was the same hotel that Max had asked her to marry him in. She walked to the desk and asked for Sheila. She was led to the spa, and, thanks to Joshua, Sheila gave her the works. A haircut and color, with highlights to lighten her auburn hair. She looked attractive and dazzling. It became more apparent when men turned to stare.

One man walked near her, and whispered, "Beautiful."

Feeling sexy and emboldened by confidence, she decided to take a leisurely walk through the hotel and window shop. She needed makeup and maybe a pair of shoes. Alex spotted Manolo Blahnik's shoe boutique and hurried in its direction. As she approached the door, she spotted Max walking out of the Chanel boutique with Corday attached to his arm. They had bags from Chanel and a small blue bag from Tiffany's, which clearly showed that they had been on a women's shopping spree.

Alex stopped in her tracks and glared at him. His gaze found her and locked on her eyes. She swirled around and ran in the direction of the taxi stand, and her tears fell hard. She forgot that she had parked her Mercedes with the attendant. Jumping into the nearest cab, she spotted Max's silver Bugatti parked on the side entrance to the hotel. "That does it. Enough of the crying, do you hear?" she said aloud, talking to give herself courage to do what she knew she should have done all along.

He is clearly enjoying his mornings and afternoons, she thought. Maybe that was how he said thank you to Corday for fucking her. He'd tied her up, let her beat him, and now he topped it off by taking that slut shopping. *It's a good job if you can get it.* Fumbling for her smartphone, she dialed Joshua's number.

"Josh, I need you to do something for me."

"Anything, Alex."

"Take me to Max's charity event."

"Sheila will be angry, but secretly she won't mind."

Her next call went to Max. "Maximilian, I can't go with you. I'll meet you at your event." She didn't want to hear any explanations. She dropped his call, and her thoughts settled on her son.

⸻ ◉ ⸻

SHE WASN'T SURE HOW and when she arrived at the apartment and into her bed. Those were lost days.

Alex lumbered out of bed and into the shower. She had not heard from Max that Thursday to explain his walking arm in arm with Corday. She expected that he would at least call to apologize and explain. But it was not in his DNA to explain or apologize to anyone about his actions, and she knew it. He had asked her to marry him. Was that one of his diabolical plots? Indeed, he was secretive about everything. What more could he be hiding?

At 7:00 p.m. the doorman notified Alex that a limo was waiting at the entrance to her apartment. She called Josh, and he answered.

"I'm already in the limo; get your ass in gear. I don't want to be late. You know I work for the guy." Alex had dressed and was ready to walk out when a loud ring came from her phone. She slid the phone out of her small, jeweled purse and peeked at the number. It was Max. No way would she answer that call. She put it on vibrate.

Josh stood by the open limo door. Slipping into the car, she noticed that Mr. Shu was driving. "Why is he here?"

"This is Blackstone's limo. I work for him, remember?"

"Does your job include being his flunky, Josh?"

"That hurts, Alex, but I'll overlook it this time. You have been so bitchy lately that I don't recognize you."

"And you have been such a traitor. Why didn't you tell me that he sent this car?"

"I don't know what's going on with you two—you hate him, you love him. You're driving me crazy."

"I'm sorry, Josh." Alex reached for Josh's hand and pulled him close, and gave him a kiss on the lips.

"You look stunning," Josh said, raising an eyebrow. "I have been seeing you in those godawful black clothes, and I didn't know that you were hiding all of that. You were right not to date me. You deserve so much more. You could marry a prince. You don't need to put up with any of Blackstone's bullshit."

"It's too late to tell me that. I'm in love with him and I should've walked away from him many times, but I didn't. I couldn't. I'm hopelessly in love with him, but I will never tell him."

Joshua and Alex rode holding each other's hands. For Josh it was sheer bliss, but for Alex the gesture was comforting and reassuring that she at least had a friend who she could depend on when times became rough, and they were about to get rough. She knew that she could not handle Max alone, especially if she decided to walk out of his life with his child.

"There he is driving that Bugatti. I would kill..." Josh paused, craned his neck, and squinted. "He has a woman in the car with him."

"Does she have dark hair?"

"Yes. She looks like you. Alex, you can't go in there the way you feel about him. I could lose my job if I decked him."

"You would do that for me, Josh?" Alex slid her hand across Josh's cheek. "Don't worry, you won't have to lose your job." They exited the limo with cameras flashing all around. The hotel was a showcase, one of his starship hotels. It was covered with LED lighting, which fitted Max's green causes. The only thing out of place was that Bugatti and that woman on his arm, Alex noted, walking into the lobby.

"It has become necessary that I speak to you," Max said in a whisper in her ear.

Alex turned, and her blue eyes glared at him. "You have nothing to say to me."

"You look beautiful. I could take you in the back and fuck you. Meet me in Conference Room B in thirty minutes."

"A slap in front of the cameras would make for a good story. They could put it right next to the one about the strangulation of the debutante."

"Meet me, please. I'll explain." Max's voice held quiet desperation in every word.

Alex and Joshua sauntered through the steel and glass doors. Blackstone and his guest slid through the doors behind them. Max proceeded to the center table below the stage, and Alex and Joshua found their seats behind his table. The girl turned and eyed Alex with an expression that was hard for Alex to figure out. Josh pulled out a chair for Alex at the same time Max pulled out a chair for the girl who was a bad copy of Alex.

Joshua whispered, "She looks nothing like you. Not even close. She can't hold a candle to you. But as usual he found some young girl to fuck."

"Stop it, Josh. I'm okay with it." Alex was okay until the announcer introduced Max's mother and father. "I thought they were dead," Alex said.

"Those people were his wards when he was a child," Josh whispered, leaning closer to her, and draping his hand around her chair. "What have you been doing lately? You haven't read a thing on your iPad. You know you can Google him."

"I like surprises." No sooner had those words left Alex's lips than the commentator introduced Max. He sauntered up the steps and onto the stage, confident and smiling. He spoke about how the environment had suffered from the overproduction of oil and the lack of wind power, and how important it was to save the wilderness and wildlife habitats for animals.

"He's wonderful." *But he's dangerous because he is such a...*

"Don't get too carried away." Josh interrupted her thoughts. "He's sitting with a woman who's trying to take your place." Josh jarred Alex into reality. She was overcome by Max's humanitarian efforts to save the environment. "Advocating saving the environment while polluting it—what a contradiction," Josh whispered.

She looked at her phone to check the time. She wasn't going to miss an opportunity to see Max. Raising her gown, she stood. "Joshua, I have to go to the ladies' room." Max's speech came to an end and the guests stood to give him a standing ovation, and he received rounds of applause.

Alex found Room B and sat waiting. She checked the time on her smartphone; she had been waiting for him for half an hour. Thinking he would not show, she headed for the double doors, when he came strutting through the side entrance.

"How has my lovely Alex been?" He stood in his black European-cut suit with a black shirt and tie, and a jacket that showed off his supremely exciting, well-toned body and long legs.

"Alex, you look fuckable, and I could eat you now if you commanded me."

"Now you're allowing me to be the Dom. That's typical of you."

"I have to apologize for the pain I've caused you."

"You can't even begin to know what I've been through. But if you would just explain, then we can go forward." Max moved closer, and his lips breezed lightly across hers. Alex swayed back, and Max caught her and laid her on the large brown leather sofa.

"What is it, Alex? What's wrong?"

"I just need you to..." Max's hand pulled up the gown and grabbed her red thong, easing it down in a second as if stripping a mannequin of her clothes for the next window dressing. His chest was moving, his breathing strong, and there was fire in his cool green eyes. She could not stop him if she wanted to, and she did not want him to stop. She inhaled and exhaled in large gasps.

Her body vibrated. Max placed his hand on her stomach, feeling the rhythm of her body. That rhythm he knew so well. He anticipated her desire for him as he passed his hand over her naked skin, stroking it with his familiar, smooth hands.

Alex's eyes went out of focus, as if in a trance as his hand wrapped around one leg and then the other. He carefully opened her legs wide, gazing between then, then he raised her legs to his shoulders and went to his knees. Looking at her vagina, he placed his finger inside slowly, and turned it in a circle. "You are wet. Tell me who is making you so wet." He pulled out his finger and extended his tongue, licking her folds one at a time.

"Only you, Max. Only you can make me hot and wasted."

Pleasure rested on Alex's face and body. She forgot about Corday lying on the couch with her legs open as wide and as inviting as she has made herself at Max's insistence. She forgot about the shopping spree. She was no longer uptight and needy, because she was being filled. Her need was being satisfied by Max. The man she wanted and would do anything to keep.

Is this the price I'll pay? Pretending that nothing ever happened? Is this the price I will pay all my life until I lose myself? she thought.

"Come for me, Alex. Come on my tongue. You're mine. There is nothing sexual we can't do together. I want all of you and I'm going to give you all of me. Now give me that orgasm."

Alex was on the precipice of reaching an orgasm when Max inserted his finger into her anus, but it was his masterful tongue on the rim of her clit that brought her to the most engrossing climax. Max stood over her, watching her face and listening to her hard breathing. She watched, unable to move as he loosened his tie and threw his jacket onto the floor.

He climbed on her, and she felt his hard body and dick press into her. Then he reached for his penis and guided it into her vagina. It took on a life of its own, knowing that Alex's vagina was home and that was where you would go when you had nowhere else to go—home, for comfort and peace.

"I'm coming, Alex."

Alex saw this as an opportunity to question him. She held him as she moved her mound into him, plowing deeper into his body, and squeezing his dick with her strong vaginal muscles. She knew that she could control his orgasms and he was greedy for her body.

"Max, did you kill that woman?"

"What kind of question is that?" With his face close to hers, she felt his brow furrow and saw a raised eyebrow.

"My need is great tonight, Alex. Don't do this to me now."

"What about Ms. Corday?"

"What about her?" He shifted to the side.

"I guess you're going to tell me that I was imagining things when I saw you on all fours with your head in that woman's cunt."

"It wasn't me. I have an alibi," he said, meeting her eyes.

"An alibi?" *Who uses those words? Someone guilty, perhaps.* "In your office and your car, and now you bring a woman to your charity event and never introduce me to your parents. Isn't 'explanation' the right word?"

"You seem to think I'm guilty of a lot of things." Max never stopped moving his body, grinding into Alex with fury. As he answered her questions, he rode her hard, up and down.

"What kind of fool do you think I am, Max? I'm getting out of here. I can't take you anymore." She pushed him off of her, pulled her dress down, and grabbed her thong. He reached for her. He touched her, and she pulled away from him. She rushed out of the conference room and the building. Max stood trying to put on his shoes and straighten his shirt and tie. After rushing out with one sleeve of his jacket on, he chased behind her, but he was too late. Alex slipped into the limo.

"Drive me home, Mr. Shu."

Chapter 3

Staring long at her beautiful dresses, her high-heel shoes, designer bags, Alex murmured, "I have no money." Hearing a loud knock and then the doorbell, she froze. *If it was Max, he would be in by now,* she thought. The doorman should have notified her. "Go to hell," she screamed. Dressed in a white silk robe with her initials, she proceeded to the door, kicking off her six-inch heels, which landed in the hall, lying around like discarded toys. "Those stay here. I have no need for them anymore," she admitted.

She opened the door to the elevator, her eyes red and wide, and her face smeared with mascara. Two men stood, relaxed, holding their badges in front of them. "Ms. Johns—or should we call you Ms. Bishop? I'm Detective Grimes and this is Detective Scotto." Detective Grimes extended his badge.

"Can we come in?"

"Yes, what is this about?" Alex said, rubbing her finger under her eyes attempting to clean the black marks left from tears but making them worse.

"Are you going somewhere?" Grimes pointed at the soft luggage Alex had dropped near the doorway leading to her bedroom.

"Yes, I had planned on going to Seattle. Please," Alex said graciously, pointing to a sofa. Detective Grimes sat. Detective Scotto, the younger of the two at about thirty, kept an eye on Alex. It wasn't a disinterested expression; it was the kind she spotted on Max's face. His glance settled firmly on Alex. She noticed him looking at her from her peripheral vision. He stood with crossed arms, head turning left and right on his six-foot frame. Wearing a cheap suit, but an expensive face, he looked like a model on the cover of *Men's Health* magazine. His hair was thick and black, his eyes deep crystal blue, and his look serious, but from the lines on his brow and near his thin lips, Alex felt that he laughed often.

Detective Grimes, a powerfully built man with a bad complexion, and soft eyes wore a gold wedding band. Alex noticed Detective Scotto's blue eyes scan the room and then survey her hair, her face, and then her body. She didn't think much of it; that was what young men did. They were attracted to young women, and since she had become comfortable with her sexuality, she was not surprised that he might be into her or at least find her mildly interesting. In a town filled with gay men, she was flattered by his attention.

Blake turned to Alex. "Ms. Johns…"

Alex interrupted, "My name is Alexander Bishop, but call me Ms. Bishop, Detective Scotto." He raised an eyebrow.

"Do you know Mr. Maximilian Blackstone?"

"What is this about?" she said, turning to Detective Grimes.

"Ms. Bishop, you haven't answered my question," Detective Scotto stated, staring at Alex.

"Wait a minute, Blake," Detective Grimes said, adjusting his body on the overstuffed sofa and bringing his gaze back to Alex. "My apologies, Ms. Bishop, but Detective Scotto is sometimes overly concerned about women and children who have been abused and especially those who have been murdered."

Alex cupped her hands and brought her hand to her mouth to bite her nails, but one look at Blake and she dropped her hand in her lap. "Yes, I know Max… I mean Mr. Blackstone." She turned and directed her statement to Blake. "I am not abused and, as you can see, I am still alive."

"This is about murder, Ms. Bishop, and if there is something that you know, I appreciate you telling us what you know now," Detective Grimes said in a commanding voice.

"I don't know anything," she said, shaking her head. "I haven't been in San Francisco long."

"It doesn't take long to get mixed up with this type of business. I hear that Mr. Blackstone is into bondage and sadomasochism," Blake said with a penetrating glance that touched the nape of Alex's neck and gave her a chill that ran down her spine.

"Mr. Scotto, it appears that you have little knowledge of BDSM."

"And you at your age are an expert?" Blake countered. "What are you, all of twenty-three or twenty-four?"

"Wait a minute. We need to return to the subject of Mr. Blackstone," Detective Grimes interrupted.

"Detective Grimes, have you spoken to Mr. Blackstone?" Alex questioned with more control.

"We haven't been able to locate him. He's a very rich man, loaded with lawyers and he is a lawyer himself. We've talked to his lawyers but didn't get much out of them."

"I think I shouldn't speak to you anymore until I get a lawyer. Please leave now."

Detective Grimes stood and shook Alex's hand. His sturdy body was held perfectly on his six-foot frame. His dark brown hair was mousy and thin, and his serious smile showed he was no-nonsense. He played by the book. He gestured to Blake that they had overstepped their bounds and their time, and Blake followed him through the foyer to the elevator door. Blake turned around and smiled. "Thanks, Ms. Bishop. I hope I wasn't too harsh with you. Just doing my job." He paused, "You are a beautiful woman, Ms. Bishop. Mr. Blackstone doesn't deserve you." He held out his card. "Call me if you hear from Mr. Blackstone. Call me if you don't. Call me, and please don't leave town." His face softened and he stood peering into Alex's eyes. Alex took the card.

"Blake, let's go," Detective Grimes stated. Blake stepped into the elevator, and it descended. "I'm worried about you. You can't get involved in this case."

"It's nothing."

"The hell if that's so. I've never seen that look in your eyes with any woman until now. It was downright sexual the way you glared at her. I thought you would fuck her there on that expensive rug. You better get a hold on yourself, Blake."

"I can handle this. You know me."

"Yes, I know you. I was a young man your age once. Every pretty woman you meet you want to fuck her, but you don't, because as an officer of the law, you know better. Take my word, if you are thinking of fucking Blackstone's woman, then you had better hand your badge over now."

"I have no plans with regards to that woman." Grimes eyed Blake as they continued walking to their black Crown Victoria. Blake knew that Grimes had seen something in his eyes. That was his tell, and he couldn't hide it from his partner. He would have to be careful, because it could cost him his job, and that was all he had. He had wanted to be a cop since he was a teen.

Stepping out of Blackstone's building, he turned and looked up. "She's sitting high up there, her and that pervert Blackstone."

"Get in the car and forget that woman if you know what's good for you. She's nothing but trouble. Have you read what people are saying about her?" Blake got behind the steering wheel and began driving away.

"All it said was that she has never had but one man in her life."

"And you're trying to be number two. You can't compete, my boy." Grimes's eyes scanned Blake's face. Blake never took his eyes off the road, but Grimes knew what Blake was thinking.

"I NEVER KILLED THAT woman."

"Which woman?" Dr. Taylor said in surprise, then reaching to his right for his pen to jot down notes.

"The woman that's linked to me in the papers."

"I thought we were discussing your sex addiction, Mr. Blackstone." Max sat up from a slumped position, opened his fist, then placed his hands in his lap, curling his fist to his mouth, and focused on the conversation. Clearly Dr. Taylor hadn't read a recent headline in the local papers, because he didn't know what Max had alluded to, but it did pique his curiosity.

"I admit..."

"No need to rush, Mr. Blackstone. You have time," Dr. Taylor said as he checked his watch.

Max swallowed hard and blew out a brisk breath of air.

"I've been a sex addict since I was very young." Dr. Taylor peered over his glasses. "When I was about ten years old, I discovered that I was highly sexual and aroused by the thought of women bound by ropes while lying across tables and chairs naked. The nature of the pictures in my mind fed into my psyche. I became so aroused by my thoughts that I would spend night and day masturbating. I began experimenting with girls older than my few years, because they were mature enough to trust with my secrets, and would not run telling their parents that I had tied them up in my tree house or tent.

"Sex with mature teen girls my age was satisfying, but when they allowed me to tie them up before I penetrated them, I found this to be more exciting than anything I had ever experienced. Later I discovered that I needed this, because they were virgins, and the moment I achieved sexual release, I had no use for them.

"Then I began to add light spankings to my list of sexual pleasures. Because of the spankings girls didn't protest. I could have a girlfriend as I entered my late teens; I was about eighteen, maybe nineteen. However, when I would request that they tie me up and whip me, they became squeamish and informed me that they could no longer date me. A mature woman entered my life. She was excited about whippings, and we dated for a time until I began to find pleasure in anal intercourse. Not all women can handle that, and I suspect that she felt that something was wrong with her, because I no longer found her vagina pleasurable. She even tried to coax me to oral sex. The problem was that once I reached my climax through my different and varied sexual experiments, I no longer found it necessary to please her. I soon learned that women expected to be satisfied as well.

"In my eagerness to please, and when I had time, I asked them to help me give them an orgasm. It was then I learned how to pleasure a woman with my tongue. I became good at it. As a matter of fact, I became so good that I could give them one orgasm after another.

"I went through virgin after virgin, but I didn't have a connection to them, and I felt that I could not bring them into my world fully, because my need for everything was too great. I would disappear to different parts of the world in search of sexual peace. It was in Thailand where I was introduced to erotic suffocation. I thought I had found the ultimate sexual thrill, but it didn't last long, so I abandoned that act. I needed a rest and decided to go home to Montana where I discovered the one woman, Alex, who would give me sexual inner peace, and become the object of my sadomasochistic love, only to lose her, because she disappeared when my attention focused on my brother, Jonas.

"Rebecca came into my life three years later. She possessed all the qualities of Alex, but she had the aggressive attitude I required that Alex seemed to lack when it came to my sexual proclivities. I could finally be free with her, so I engaged in all my sexual desires, and it was going great. My business soared, I was able to rest at night, and I had never felt better until she wanted more.

"I tried to explain that I could not commit to a relationship with her, because I was in love with Alex. I discovered that Alex and Rebecca were the same person."

"Incredible," interrupted the therapist. He straightened his shoulders and leaned forward, his eyes focused on Max. Max had gotten his attention. "Mr. Blackstone, as much as I would like to continue this session, I have another patient waiting. I need to hear about Rebecca and Alex. There is something there that needs exploring. We will resume your therapy next week. We will continue where you've left off."

Max walked out of the office and received an urgent message from his security advisor to return to his office immediately.

⎯⎯◉⎯⎯

ALEX HAD TO HAVE A drink. She hadn't signed on for this—police coming into her apartment and telling her that she couldn't leave town. *They tell that to everyone,* she thought. She wouldn't listen; they hadn't charged her with anything. There was no way in hell she believed that Max could have killed that woman or wanted to. But the position she saw Mr. Black and that Ms. Corday in made her sad. *How could he?* she thought. "I loved him so much and I would have done anything for him. I just wanted him to be true to me. That bastard!" she screamed from her terrace. *He had the nerve to bring a woman to his fundraiser after asking me.* "I hate him. I love him," she whispered.

It was hard to pick up her feet. She planted one foot and then the other, heading to the fridge to get another drink. She opened a Heineken. Walking to the terrace, and looking down, she guzzled it down from the bottle. She didn't know what to do. She heard the buzz from the intercom. She ran back inside and hit the buzzer.

"Yes, what is it?"

"I have a present for you, Ms. Johns." She hated that name. But it would be confusing to change it now. Maybe she needed time to come up with an excuse to use her real name, like getting the hell out of there.

"Send it up." She walked in a circle. "What the fuck is it now, and who is it from?"

She knew the answer, and she became angry.

"Ms. Johns, I just received this. It looks fancy." The doorman handed her a small, wrapped box tied with a blue-and-gold ribbon. She set the box on the table and pulled out the card:

My darling Alex,

I know this necklace can't make up for everything I have put you through, such as not explaining about Ms. Corday, which is unforgivable, and that woman who accompanied me to the fundraiser, but I had to be in Japan early. I purchased this for you and am instructing my secretary to send it to you. I didn't have time to tell you about my flight. I will see you shortly. I hope this necklace will make you smile and correct the misunderstandings you may have about me. Wear it and think of me.

Your loving Max

First she held the card to her heart. "Oh, Max, I love you so much. You are such a fucking pervert, but I still love you. What am I going to do with you?" Anger covered her in waves.

Alex wondered if he thought that giving her presents would blind her to what she'd seen in his office. She could stand his desire for that kind of sexual arousal, because she had learned to enjoy it, and she felt that their lives would be enriched because they had been exclusive to each other, but when she was confronted with another woman taking her place, it was beyond the pale, and she couldn't tolerate it for one more minute.

She threw the box on the sofa, walked to the kitchen, made herself a sandwich, placed it on a plate, and opened up another bottle of beer. She decided to see what his fucked-up present looked like. Tearing the paper off and dropping the ribbon on a table, she opened the box and gasped.

It was a yellow diamond necklace to match her engagement ring, with six large teardrops, each surrounded by white diamonds. "Where am I going to wear this?" She held it to her neck. "My God, this must have cost a small fortune."

Alex had an idea. It wasn't brilliant, but she hadn't had a brilliant idea since she'd met Max.

"I'll fix him. I'll sell it, send back his engagement ring, and use the money from the necklace to get an apartment until I can get the hell out of San Francisco. I'll go home to Seattle, get a job, take care of my son, and never see his fucked-up ass again. He can strangle the next woman crazy enough to want him and get involved in his lifestyle. Everyone makes a mistake, and I still have time to correct mine," she murmured.

Alex's personal phone rang. "Ms. Bishop?"

"Yes, this is Ms. Bishop."

"This is Detective Blake Scotto."

"What can I do for you, Detective? I've already told you that I don't know anything, and I would need to speak to my lawyer."

"I noticed that there is a restaurant near your apartment, and I was wondering whether I could buy you dinner." There was a long silence.

"If you're trying to get information about Blackstone, you have come to the wrong person."

"This is not about Blackstone."

"Then what is this about?"

"I saw that you had been crying and I thought that you may need someone to talk to."

"I don't know you, Detective Scotto, and I'm not about to cry on a stranger's shoulders. If I need a shoulder to cry on, I'll get a dog."

"I just thought that you needed someone. I just wanted to be friends."

"That's impossible at this time. Like I said, I'll get a dog."

"Well, that didn't sound as if you would never consider it. That sounds promising."

"Take it whatever way you want, but I'm busy now, and I have to go. Goodbye, Detective Scotto."

"Call me Blake." Blake managed to get out these few words before the call dropped.

Chapter 4

Max returned to the fundraiser to support the environment after washing up and putting on his tie. He shook hands and smiled, but his heart was with Alex. He received the usual pat on the back and a "good job" from the prominent donors, said his goodbyes and dropped his date at home.

He entered his penthouse with the glorious view of San Francisco and the bridge lit with LED lightning, which he had long advocated. He sat in his chair on his terrace, placed his feet on a table, lit a cigar, raised his head, blew out some smoke, and leaned back. His manservant brought him a glass of wine. He lay out in the open air to feel the chill of the night. He didn't remember when he had felt so cold, but the heat in his body warmed him. The peaceful night calmed him, and he began to think about how his life had been so hectic as to send him fleeing to his retreat in Montana.

Max had thought a week at his lodge in Billings would provide respite from the hellish month he had dealing with business and his brother, Jonas. Millions were wasted to buy Jonas's freedom. It had been one thing after another with Jonas, and Max had taken the brunt of the criticism by allowing the press to think it was him involved in so many embarrassing situations with women.

First it was the marriage in Las Vegas. Jonas married a young girl, barely sixteen. Max had to pay off her parents to keep them from pressing charges and charging Jonas as a pedophile, and the annulment had cost Max dearly, because he had to sell some stock to bail Jonas out of that mess.

Then it was the stripper in Las Vegas. She and her boyfriend drugged Jonas, and he married her under Max's name. All Jonas's marriages, the weddings and divorces, were in Max's name not Jonas Blackstone. Max spent millions to keep his name and the fact that he had a twin out of the papers. The last scandal was a woman who had been found dead in one of Max's apartments. But this time it was a woman to whom he had been engaged.

Max owned all the assets he received from their parents' deaths, all the hotels from Vegas to Macao. Jonas had pissed away every dime of his inheritance, and now he was coming for whatever Max had sacrificed—his love life, marriage, and reputation—to keep.

Business and his brother's love was his single focus. Even though he shelled out millions on Jonas's antics, Max was able to keep most of his fortune and turn it into billions, but at the rate Max was covering Jonas's ass, he would be broke soon.

He didn't have the inclination or the strength to keep up the schedule of flying all over the world, so he enlisted Jonas. After all, Jonas was consuming most of his wealth. Max didn't have the time to spend it. He wanted a family, he wanted a life, and he wanted out of the BDSM lifestyle that held sway over him. He was getting deeper and deeper into it, and he saw himself drowning.

⚬

JONAS WAS INSTRUMENTAL in introducing him to Sophia. It was the night Max flew into Vegas and found Jonas at his hotel, impersonating him. He walked in on his brother and a girl in his penthouse suite.

"What the fuck, Jonas? I leave to get some rest and find you in my room with your dick up this young woman's ass and you wearing a collar." He walked to the restroom, retrieved a robe, and threw it over the teen's body.

"Wait, big brother, it's not what you think," Jonas said, peeking to the side at Max, never bothering to stop fucking and never bothering to show any shame.

"That's always the answer I get from you, and then it's exactly what I think."

"She's my wife."

"Good Lord, Jonas, can't you see she's a teenager?" Jonas wiped his eyes and pulled his dick out. He gestured for the doe-eyed girl to leave the room. Jonas stood watching as the girl walked out of Max's bedroom and into one of the nearest bedrooms.

"Damn, that ass is tight," Jonas said, turning away from Max and staring at the girl.

"And couldn't you do that in another room besides mine? There are five other bedrooms."

"You never sleep, and you are never here." He shrugged his shoulders and twisted his mouth. "I didn't think—"

Max cut into his conversation. "You never think," Max said, opening his safe.

"Well, not that you would come in this time of morning." He carelessly dismissed what Max had said. "I don't have any money and when you have so much..."

"And that's a good reason to impersonate me. I could be charged as a pedophile and lose my liquor and hotel license. My reputation is already shot to hell because of you. If I lose everything, then what?" His brow furrowed and eyes narrowed, he turned and faced Jonas.

Jonas strutted naked to the hidden bar and hit a button, then poured himself a drink. Max looked at him with the palm of his hand resting across his mouth, shaking his head, and remembering that Jonas never took anything seriously—not money, not Max, and not even his own life.

"Put some clothes on, Jonas, and get that little girl out of here. I haven't slept in two days." Jonas retrieved his pants from the floor. Max watched him, knowing that the crumpled slacks had been pulled and tossed in a hurry. His shirt appeared to have been torn from his body because buttons were scattered on the bed and floor. After stepping into his trousers and remaining shirtless, Jonas reached into his pants pocket.

"I know what you need." Jonas pulled out his iPhone and began texting.

Jonas: Sophia I need u ASAP at Blackstone Casino Hotel.

Soph: Hi, Jon what's in it for me?

Jonas: My rich brother. He hasn't slept in days & hasn't fucked a woman in years.

Soph: Then I think handcuffs and whips are in order. I'll bring some toys just in case. (:

"What the fuck are you doing, Jonas? I'm trying to have a serious conversation with you."

Jonas tucked his iPhone back into a pocket. "I just ordered you a woman."

"I don't need a woman. I need a family," Max said, picking up Jonas's shirt and tossing it on a bench.

"She's not any woman. She can help you sleep. And you don't have to take medication that quack has been prescribing you." He walked to Max's closet and selected two suits and two pairs of black shoes. "These are just my style," he said, caressing the suits as he would a woman. "You never wear them." He checked the price. "They still have tags." Jonas pulled the tag off one suit and glanced at it.

"Speaking of medication, have you taken yours?" Max peered at Jonas with a raised eyebrow. He followed Jonas into his large closet. "So now you're shopping in my closet, and taking my clothes along with my name." Jonas either didn't hear Max, or chose to ignore the remark about his medication. As a child he had been diagnosed as hyperactive and a host of other psychological problems stemming from their parents' deaths. Max remained hopeful that he would grow out of his conditions, but they appeared to worsen after he was released from the army.

Jonas turned to Max with two suits draped across his arm. "You have better taste than I do, and these are for a job well done," he said with a quick smile, sauntering up to the cabinet and picking through Max's ties. "And besides, I can't afford those suits or these ties." He laid the blue silk tie on the suit to determine if the color would match.

"Those two suits cost about ten thousand each," Max stated, following behind Jonas.

"What's the matter, brother? Are you having problems with your oil wells, or is it the casinos and hotels that are losing money?" Jonas gave a quick grin, dropped his pants, and strutted into the shower.

Max eyed the teenage girl, sitting in a chair in a yellow floral cotton dress with her legs crossed. She reminded him of an innocent lost girl. He could see her charm, but he couldn't understand how Jonas, at his age, would find anything in common with her.

Her mouth moving gingerly, chewing gum, she glanced up at him. "Shit, man, you two look like twins. I can't tell you apart."

"We are twins." He walked past her, plopping down into a beige silk floral wingback chair. "Tell me, how long have you known Jonas?"

"Counting today..." She glanced up and around the room, shaking her head from left to right. "About a week."

"When did you two marry?"

"Oh... the first day we saw each other. We were both high... I mean drunk, and it just seemed to be a natural thing to do."

She pulled out her phone and began texting. She never glanced up until she saw Jonas standing in front of her. "Come on, baby doll. We have places to go and people to see," Jonas said with a quick, gleeful smile.

Max reached for Jonas's arm, looking at the teen, then he said, "Wait here, baby doll; Jonas will be with you shortly." He led Jonas by the arm into his room and shut the door.

"What the fuck is wrong with you? You know that child a week, and you marry her?"

"Well, she wouldn't give it up until she was married. Who would have thought that I would find a virgin these days?"

"Damn it, Jonas, she's a virgin, because she's barely sixteen. She's a minor, and you're broke."

"That reminds me, I need some money to take her back to Iowa."

"How much is it this time?" Max said with a huff, then picked up his checkbook on his desk and wrote Jonas a check. "I don't want to see my forged signature on any more checks," he said, looking up. "You need to ask for what you want. One day..."

"Can't you see I'm changing? I asked you, didn't I?" Jonas sauntered to Max's desk and took the check with a small grin. "I need cash too."

Max reached into his open safe and handed Jonas a stack of bills. Jonas took the money with his head and eyes lowered.

Max never saw Jonas until he was broke or claimed he was looking for a job. He missed his brother, because that was all the family he had. But missing Jonas had cost him dearly.

"When are you going to take responsibility for your life and stop meddling in mine and causing trouble for me and yourself?" Max questioned Jonas with a steely glance. This was always their conversation.

"I suppose you blame me for those rotten women that you have found all on your own? I just showed you that they were no good for you," Jonas commented.

"You went out of your way to set Rachel up with a man and a woman," Max said, eyeing Jonas.

"But if she was devoted to you, she wouldn't have taken that offer." That was Jonas's answer, and it hadn't changed. *Maybe Jonas is right*, Max thought. But it wasn't up to him to decide anything that had to do with Max's life.

Jonas stuffed the check and money into his pocket, reached for the girl's hand, and led her to the elevator. "You're taking my Louis Vuitton bag?" Max threw up his hands in disgust.

"I left you that other ridiculously priced one. You can afford it. I can't. How would it look for people to think that I'm you and I have that tattered old leather satchel?"

"It would look just fine to me," Max shouted.

"See you, big brother." And the elevator closed.

When Jonas left, the concierge called Max, reminding him that a woman by the name of Sophia was waiting. He hesitated with his hand covering his mouth. "Oh, what the hell. It can't be any worse than staying up for two days and finding a naked teenager in your room." He relented. "Send her up to my suite, Carlos."

———⚬———

IT WAS WITH SOPHIA that Max could be detached and not form a relationship. It was with Sophia that he experimented with the idea of Dom and sub. Sophia would play the sub because she enjoyed humiliation. It was with Sophia that he could sleep that night. He would spank her on every occasion and learned to enjoy their sessions, but he stayed in control and never allowed any physical or sexual intimacy. That was until he met Alex and Rebecca.

He didn't have time to cultivate a relationship; relationships were demanding, and what woman would follow him around the world at a minute's notice and wait for him in a hotel room six days a week? That kind of woman was not what he wanted. He wanted a woman who would be his—a woman who knew his secrets and would accept him and love him.

For this type of woman, if he was lucky enough to find her, he wanted to be the first and the last man she would know.

Max needed a woman who could fill many desires, because he had plenty. His cup of need was empty, and it would take an ocean to fill it.

His desires had been growing greater and greater, but the women had been less and less giving. He was spending more time at his hotels in Hong Kong when clearly he needed to be home to rein in his brother. How could he sleep when he didn't know what Jonas would do from one day to the next?

After a session with Sophia, Max lay down naked and stretched across his bed. He had not planned on falling asleep, but surprisingly he had. The session, as he called it, worked, and he woke as refreshed as if he had been on a vacation and had done nothing but rest.

The service Sophia provided was invaluable. He thought that he should have been doing this sooner. What could be wrong with trying to get some sleep when he needed it? He wasn't putting medicine into his body. As a matter of fact, pills didn't appear to work for him anymore, but BDSM seemed to provide what he needed.

Even after a good night's sleep he had been jolted by a call. The call came from his lawyer.

"What is it now, Bradley?"

"Max, you know I wouldn't call you on frivolous matters, but it's Jonas again."

"What? He just left here. He had his wife with him."

"Did anyone tell him that it was illegal to marry a fifteen-year-old girl?" Bradley stated, outraged.

"I knew the girl was a little too young, but I never imagined that she was only fifteen. I didn't think he was that stupid, picking up a child. For fuck's sake, he's thirty. Bradley, I've gone over that with Jonas..."

"Yeah... me too. Jonas's reply was, 'she looked older.' That's just not going to fly in a court of law. No judge is going to go for that excuse, and he married her under an assumed name. It gets better."

"Don't keep me guessing."

"All this was done under your name." There was a long silence, and then Bradley heard glass shatter. Max had thrown the glass against the wall, because he could not believe that Jonas had broken his promise. He had allowed Jonas to go to meetings in the States while assuming his identity whenever he had important business in Europe or Asia. Jonas saw this as an opportunity to steal his identity.

"What can I do?" He exhaled.

"Pull out your checkbook and hope her parents are greedy and a little less pious, otherwise, you're screwed."

Calling his secretary, Max decided to go to Montana to ski and fish, and forget.

"Make arrangements for my jet to take me to Billings and tell my valet to pack my ski clothes. Have some of my employees accompany me. I'm not in the mood to be alone."

"Yes, Mr. Blackstone. Should I arrange to have a young woman available? Ms. Corday would love to spend the weekend if you need her for anything."

"No, I have to clear my head—too many complications—and I may have to fly back to San Francisco, and she is needed in the office."

After arriving in Billings, Max departed his jet and decided to check on his hotel staff and stay a night there. "Driver, take us to my lodge; I think I want to do some skiing before I go to my home."

The driver turned in the direction of Blackstone Lodge. The snow hadn't fallen that day. It was sunny, and a splash of sun on his face made him feel different. He exited his limo with his young staff leading the way. That was the day he set eyes on the most appealing young woman he had ever seen.

I can't believe that such a woman exists, Max thought. *I have to say something to her, but what? I've never come across a woman that I'm physically and sexually drawn to. I don't have the skills to deal with this kind of problem. I want her and I can't take no for an answer. But what will I do if she turns me down? She's not like the typical girls hunting for a rich bachelor. She looks different. She doesn't know who I am or doesn't care. That turns me on. I have to say something.*

Watching Alex as she walked ahead of him made him anxious, and whenever he became anxious he didn't act like the confident man he had always been. He had never felt an automatic attraction to any woman until now. He didn't know what made him lust after this young woman, but he felt it throughout his body. He felt it in his head, and most of all he felt it in his manhood. The pulsating feeling that coursed its way from his chest downward took on its own life. He had no control, and he didn't want to control that feeling that had once been dormant.

Max let the feeling take him and lead him. He had always been in control, but not now. It felt liberating to go wherever his passion led him.

He couldn't believe his body. It caused him to turn and speak when normally he waited for a woman to approach him. He never waited long. This young woman, however, appeared to be running from him, and he, being the alpha male, would not let her get away. She was his for the taking, and he would corner her and run her down until she was his.

Listening to his mind, he couldn't believe that he thought of her as his. He was a man who would play with his competition until he got what he wanted, and then he would leave nothing of them once he obtained their companies. He would fire the employees and dismantle the company, coldly. But today he felt his heart beating and he didn't know whether he liked this or not. It didn't feel natural to him; there was too much warmth. And that meant that sooner or later he would lose.

He was taken by her innocence and her blue-saucer eyes. Her full, pouty lips, her warm, tender face, and the way she walked—gliding with natural confidence.

Not wanting to let her get away, he had to speak to her. All he managed was something about her necklace. But his eyes naturally strayed downward, and when he met her glance she noticed that he had his eyes on her breasts.

He couldn't help thinking that he wanted to see more of her, so he arranged a meeting with his staff at his home, and he stole away, intending to walk through the doors the next day and get her alone so that he could ask her out.

He wanted to say, *"Ms. Bishop, if it is at all possible, could you have dinner tomorrow night?"* He practiced over and over what he would say, but when he met her at the hotel desk, he stumbled over his words and all he could manage was, "I would like to see you." Alex must have thought him a fool, or that he wanted to fire her.

He couldn't forgive himself for placing his brother ahead of the woman he desired above all else—Alex. The sound of the helicopter over his terrace jarred him from distasteful memories, and he smiled when he thought of the day he had met Alex.

Chapter 5

Max couldn't spend his days looking after a fuck-up like Jonas, especially when he acted as if he would never grow up. Even when Max had cut him off, he would manage to get money by forging checks in Max's name.

All of this was eating at Max when he spotted Alex, a cute young woman that tugged at his heart the minute he had locked eyes on her. He hadn't dated in years. He was never good at it, and he didn't know what to say to Alex, because she looked all of twenty and he was thirty. What was he going to tell her? *I have been watching you*, he thought. *No, it sounds as if I'm a stalker. She would probably call the police.*

What could they discuss? Do you like Bach, Beethoven, or The Black Eyed Peas? *Maybe she likes country and western or hip-hop. That's no good. Can I take you to the opera? Another stupid idea. Maybe it would be better to fuck her and forget her.* He found her too desirable for that. What was his alternative, spending his life with women he would pay to whip him for a good night's sleep?

He could pretend to be a quiet, silent type, and then introduce himself. He felt that she was interested.

Max walked cautiously to the counter, no longer displaying his confident stride—head up, eyes focused, his trademark in the boardroom. He had to appear confident for his sake; after all, he was Maximilian Blackstone the head of Blackstone Enterprises. But seeing Alex made him nervous and unsure of himself, and that was why he dropped the ball and sounded like an idiot when he said, "Can I see you?" He flubbed that line. And she looked at him as if he was mentally challenged.

Even knowing the difficulties and time it took to cultivate a relationship, he still wanted this relationship, and he would put in the time no matter how long it took.

Max fell in love.

He didn't know why it happened; it just did. It was her eyes, her mouth, her body, and that unsophisticated way she carried herself and her simple off-the-rack clothes that turned him on. He needed to relax and forget the stress, and she presented a diversion.

It was by accident that he met her on the slopes the next day, trying to ski. He could tell that she was a novice, and all he had to do was hide and watch her, which provided entertainment for him. He made the wrong move when he walked behind her, but he couldn't resist her beautiful little ass just protruding in the air, begging for something to be done. He moved closer to her and felt compelled to ease even closer.

It didn't occur to him that she might be insulted by his antics; he just plowed ahead. After all, he was Maximilian Blackstone. Women would send nude pictures and underwear to his room as if he was a rock star whenever he strutted into his hotels. They were women looking for a rich husband or boyfriend, and he knew it. So that was why he took his chances, only to be told by Alex to leave her alone.

He walked away with his feelings hurt, but as luck would have it—and he always had a certain amount of luck—she fell, and he was there to scoop her up and deposit her into his arms and into his bed.

Just when he knew that Alex was the one he wanted to share his life with, a call came from his lawyer early in the morning. It was a problem with Jonas again.

"Mr. Blackstone."

"Yes, do you know what time it is?" he said, gazing at Alex, sound asleep after meds and a round of sexual intercourse that cured what ailed him.

"Yes, it's 3 a.m., but you said to call if Jonas is in trouble."

"What is it this time?"

"Another woman, sir."

"I'll be there in an hour."

Max glanced over at Alex. There she was, lying in his bed. How did he get so lucky with such a pretty, fresh woman? He remembered the day he arrived at Blackstone Lodge and her wide blue eyes stopped him in his tracks.

Now he had to leave his woman and look after his brother, who would not give him a moment's peace. As he walked into the hot shower he thought of Alex and what he would say to her. He wrote her a note. He was in a hurry and jotted down a few words. As soon as he had written it he wanted to tear it up, but he didn't have time to write another, so he let it stand.

After reaching his private plane and settling down, he realized that the note was plain stupid. "Why did I write that?" he said. "What kind of man says that he had a fortuitous meeting with a woman he adores?" He sat and wrote another letter, thinking that after dealing with Jonas, he would give it to Alex with a large bouquet of roses.

My dearest Alex,

I have never been in love before until now. I know it is presumptuous of me to assume that you feel the same way that I do. If you will give me time, I will prove to you in every possible way that I love you and that I will try to make you happy. I have met many women in my thirty years, and I know the difference between you and them. I don't want to lose you. Please wait for me and you will never be sorry.

Loving you,

Max

This was the letter he should have written. Folding it, he eased it into his inside suit pocket and closed his eyes, chasing sleep, but it would not come because he was worried about Jonas.

Bradley informed Max that Jonas had been found in a hotel room in Las Vegas with two unsavory characters, one a stripper and the other a card shark. Jonas had signed in as Maximilian Blackstone. The maid entered the room and found the five-thousand-dollar-a-night suite at the Aria Resort and Casino trashed. And lying on the floor were the stripper, the card shark, and Jonas—with drugs lying underneath him.

With what appeared to be a drug overdose, Jonas was taken to a nearby hospital. The police reported that it was Max and called his lawyer. They were going to arrest Jonas for drug possession and for destruction of private property. It was a mess that only Max could sort out and take care of. He begged his lawyers to see about Jonas, but they would have no part of it. Max wanted to stay with Alex and never think about the hellish world that he found himself in because of a fucked-up twin brother.

He flew out on his private jet and landed in Las Vegas.

At the hospital he walked into the room with a proposal. "If you don't get yourself together, then that's it. I'm going to put money up for you to open your own business. I don't care what it is. Just do something and stop this crazy behavior."

"Glad to see you too, bro."

"And don't call me that."

"What do you want me to say? What do you want from me?" Jonas said with apologetic eyes.

"I want you to grow up and take care of yourself and stop being an embarrassment."

"So that's all I am to you, an embarrassment? I'm not an embarrassment when I take your place at your business meetings."

"You receive a handsome check for your troubles, after which you are broke the next day. Yes, you are an embarrassment." Max turned his back and walked to the desk and filled out the necessary papers.

After signing him out of the hospital, Max brought him to his penthouse suite. After one day Jonas was back to his old tricks and searching for the stripper once more. After finding her in a seedy hotel room off the strip, he finally came to his senses and called Max, who was returning to Montana.

"Max."

"What the hell do you want now, Jonas?"

"I can't keep doing this, Max."

"You've just discovered this? I was wondering what it would take for you to come to your senses."

"If you help me one last time, you won't regret it."

"For God's sake, Jonas, I'm headed back to Montana. I left something there."

"Is it a woman?" Jonas asked slyly.

"Why?"

"Because I found a letter in your suit, and it was addressed to Alex. Well, brother, if it's a man, I just want you to know that I don't judge."

"For fuck's sake, Jonas, it's a woman. And I don't care whether you judge me or not. Put my letter down and stay out of my clothes. I'll get there as soon as I can."

⸻ ◆ ⸻

MAX DIRECTED THE PILOT to turn his jet around and pick up Jonas, who had to leave Nevada. His private jet then headed for San Francisco. Max got to his feet, walking to the back of the plane, where he sat and made a call to Alex.

"Let me speak to Alex."

"Mr. Blackstone, Ms. Bishop left this morning with one of your employees from the Lodge."

"Who was it, a man or a woman?"

"It was a young man, sir, in a Volvo."

"Thank you, I'll take care of it."

Max made another call to his lodge.

"Check and see if Joshua is at the front desk." He waited a minute.

"No, sir."

"Can you get me his private phone number?"

"I'll call you back, sir."

Max turned the phone off and stared out of the window.

"Bro. Hey, bro, the food is great, and the wine is fabulous. Remind me to travel with you more often," Jonas said, eating with his head down, never looking up from his plate, until he looked back to see Max staring down and not eating. "What's wrong, Max?"

"What...? Oh, nothing."

"Something is wrong. You can tell me." Max's phone rang and he answered it.

"Mr. Blackstone." Max reached for his pen and paper and wrote down a number; then, with a huff, he placed the pen down.

"Try to find her, will you? I'll reach Billings tomorrow at 4 p.m. I hope you have some news for me then."

Max walked and sat near Jonas. "Look, I need time away from you. I have spent my life trying to take care of you at the expense of my own happiness. This has got to end. I want you to find something that you can do and get you out of my hair. I will put up the money until you start making money. What do you say?"

Jonas glared at him and then said, "You are really crazy about that Alex. I have never done anything for you, big brother. I'll stay out of trouble and make my own way if you help me." They hugged and shook hands.

He made Jonas a proposition. If Jonas found a business that he thought he could run and be interested in, then Max would support him until it brought in money. That business was Pandora's Retreat, and to Max's astonishment it brought in more money with barely any overheads. Jonas had made many connections impersonating Max and he felt no compunction in using them. He developed an advertisement and sold it to the superrich executives. It was sold as a retreat to rest, relax, and discover your inner self. Nevertheless, it was what it was, and it did not matter how he dressed it up or gave a fancy name to it—it was a place where bondage was practiced.

To Max's and Jonas's surprise, men from all walks of life and industries came through Pandora's doors. The place was advertised as discreet, and it was for everyone except Jonas, who kept their secrets until they became competitors for Max's business.

After Max helped Jonas, then he figured that he could concentrate on Alex. But when he arrived in Montana, he discovered that Alex had disappeared, and no one would divulge her whereabouts to him. He learned that her résumé was fabricated. He didn't have time to concentrate on finding her just yet, because his hotels were losing money and there was trouble with his oil wells and the politicians on his payroll.

His business ventures and Jonas's lifestyle had consumed his time. One day he woke, it was three years later, and his life was getting progressively worse. He hadn't had a date or met a girl since he left Alex to take care of Jonas.

It was Jonas who impersonated Max one day, ordering his staff to hire Max a sub for his office.

———⧓———

"GOOD MORNING," JONAS said, walking up to the secretary's desk and handing her a present with flowers. He stood wondering why Max had never bothered to mention her. Then he realized that she was not Max's type, but she was his—a woman who would be impressed by a rich man. He called her into Max's office.

"Ms. Corday, please come to my office. I have something very important that I need."

She walked in and spied this handsome man who was her boss. All of a sudden he was warm and pleasant and all hands-on after being cold and aloof.

"Please sit," Jonas said, patting the leather sofa cushion next to him that he was sitting on. "I have questions I would like to ask you, and if you answer them correctly, you will get a big bonus in your next paycheck. Do you find me handsome?"

"Yes, of course, Mr. Blackstone."

"Would you consider dating me?"

She thought for a minute. Was this a test? She peered at Jonas and spied a teasing grin. He was serious. "Yes, I would. What woman would turn you down?"

"Would you consider fucking me here in my office?" Another pause.

"I'd fuck you anywhere, Mr. Blackstone," Corday said with a wide grin, and she sat at the corner of the sofa.

"Then come closer," Jonas said, leaning on one hand in her direction. He let his hand lie on the hem of her skirt. Turning his head to the side in perfect silence, he rested his right hand on her knee. He moved it between her thighs, then up and up, and to his surprise she had no underwear on. He could not believe his good luck. He fingered her clit, and her head fell back, and her mouth opened wide, and the breathing became intense. He felt Ms. Corday moisten.

"My dear, have you ever had anal intercourse?"

"Of course, hasn't everyone?"

"My kind of girl," Jonas whispered. He pulled her to the floor, and she rested her breasts on the edge of the sofa. She waited, and Jonas searched around his pocket for a latex. He never left home without one. He believed in being prepared, especially since he had a fetish for a good ass and Ms. Corday had the best he had seen in his years of abusing them.

Jonas hurried and pulled his pants down and took off his shirt. Then he kicked off his shoes and he was ready. He rolled the latex on his hard penis and then he rubbed Corday's glistening, tanned butt. He knew how to massage an ass until it fell asleep. He took the head of his dick and rimmed it around the eye of the anus and slowly inserted it until it was in. And since she had confessed that she was not a novice to anal intercourse, it would be a cinch to have his orgasm and get out quickly.

Chapter 6

Jonas kept out of trouble for a year and managed to set up Pandora's Retreat where, to all appearances, he enjoyed the title of businessman. His retreat advertised to all who craved the kind of lifestyle that he thought people were looking to achieve—hanging out, hooking up, S&M, and bondage.

He spent many days and nights making the place a success. He even brought in Sophia to assist in running the club. Sophia had a large clientele of bankers, lawyers, and some of the very rich in San Francisco and Los Angeles who wanted to remain anonymous.

Jonas continued to use Max's name and not tell anyone that he was the twin brother. That was how one day he met a young woman at a black-and-white ball and fell in love. Instead of owning up to his true self, he introduced himself as Maximilian Blackstone. *No one cares about Jonas*, he thought. He was just another loser to his rich, successful, and well-known brother.

"Hi, I'm Max."

"I'm Kathy Van DeMeer."

"Yes, I know your father. He's that billionaire newspaper man."

"And you are that billionaire Maximilian Blackstone."

"How did you know?"

"Someone pointed you out. See that woman over there? Wave. She is responsible for our meeting. Very seldom do I meet a man my own age who is not married," Kathy said with a sigh.

"Do tell. And what age are you? I'm twenty-five."

"I'm thirty—not exactly your age."

"Close enough. A man as handsome as you, one would think that you would be taken by now."

"I guess I'm a moving target. You know what they say about moving targets."

"Yeah, they are much harder to hit."

"But you will not have a hard time nailing me. I'm yours already."

Kathy looped her hand under Jonas's arm, and they strolled out to the terrace grounds. He placed her near a hedge and lifted her long black satin gown. He was surprised to find that she had no panties on, and her mound was bald. *Is there a shortage of material for underwear, or am I missing something?* he thought. Breathing hard at the feel of her bald mound, he pressed his body next to hers. He pushed his body into her, and she met the feel of his hard dick through his pants. She didn't say a word, but looked up at him with her large blue eyes, and he cupped his mouth over hers. The kisses were hard; the kisses were violent. Their breathing was strong and increasingly heavy.

"Are you going to stand there with my dress hoisted up, or are you going to fuck me now?"

Surprised at her forward and unsuspecting lack of modesty, Jonas unzipped his tuxedo pants, and Kathy pulled his hard dick out and put it in position to enter her. She guided him in as she placed his large hand around her small neck. "Keep your hand there as you fuck me. It's so much better like this," she insisted. "This is great isn't it?"

"Yes. Yes," Jonas cried out over and over, his tall body contorting and bending to meet her petite form.

"Max, I've heard about you. I want to be your pupil. I want to experience a life of bondage."

Jonas was intrigued and surprised. He liked Kathy, but sooner than later he would have to admit his true identity. He decided it would be later.

LOOKING FOR MORE CLIENTS and finding out that Kathy had inherited a large trust fund in the seven-figure range, Jonas decided to mix business with pleasure. Still pretending to be Max, he called Kathy.

"Kathy, I know that I refused to bring you to Pandora's Retreat, but only because I didn't want you to be turned off by my lifestyle. It's not something that you do when you're bored."

"I assure you, Max, I am well aware of the dangers, especially if I do not engage in it with someone who knows what they are doing. That's why when I heard that you owned Pandora's I wanted to be a part of it. Not only that, but I can bring you clients."

Jonas perked up, knowing that this could mean big business. He could demonstrate to Max that he could run a business and stay focused, and pay Max back for all the money lost on him.

"Max—" Kathy said, "—can you personally show me around the place? I hear that you have apartments on the grounds. That sounds delicious and private."

"I'll pick you up at 1 p.m. We can make a day of it. I can see what you know," Jonas said, raising his fist like a child that had just won his favorite sport.

"Oh, that sounds terrific. A day with you and a little BDSM all in one day makes me a little excited. Bring all your toys." Kathy's eager voice sounded like a child going on a play date without her mother.

"Don't worry. Each room is filled with everything we need."

The thought that Kathy was a novice crossed his mind when he first met her, but now he was having second thoughts. She sounded as if she knew the ins and outs of this life and maybe more than he suspected.

Chapter 7

A jolt of sun and cool air stirred Max and he woke. He had been thinking and dreaming of Alex, Jonas, and Maxim. That morning he flew to Seattle in search of his son. By now Alex was determined not to allow him access to their child.

His limo stopped in Seattle's old district. The houses were pre-war era, each painted in white with a front porch. It was a neighborhood of families where children and grandchildren were watched over by grandparents.

The grandparents were the sort that had survived their hippie days in San Francisco and had returned to Seattle after years of drugs and war to make a living and raise children as rebellious as they had once been. What they could not give their children, they were now prepared to heap on their grandchildren. Love and protection were exhibited all along the streets where little girls and boys played freely without a care, because someone was always looking out for their safety.

Max's thoughts settled on his and Jonas's childhood experiences. They were privileged in one way and poor in another. Their guardians sent them off to military schools and boarding schools at a very young age. There were always nannies, housekeepers, and maids.

This would not be the fate of his son, he vowed. Although Alex refused to answer his texts or calls, he would put all his business on hold to find his son. He hoped that he could locate Alex as well.

At Max's insistence, his driver made two passes by the clapboard house before he spied a man coming through a screen door. The man, about sixty, had a full head of white hair and carried a small red-and-yellow car down the stairs with a young child trailing on his heels. It was an old, beat-up red and yellow plastic car, which had pedals. He could imagine that it once belonged to Alex when she was a child. He heard the child say, "Put it down, Grandpa. I want to ride."

"Alright, Maxim, but Gramps can't push you for very long."

"I know."

Tears welled in Max's eyes; he wanted to be the one watching over him, but he wasn't ready to meet his son, not with tears in his eyes.

He watched for a moment. "Drive on," Maximilian said with a small sigh. Then he leaned back in his seat in complete silence.

How could Alex separate him from his son? *Maybe she thinks it is a better environment to have her parents raise little Maxim*, he thought. His mind was conflicted. How could it be good to separate a child from their father and mother? But then he thought about the type of environment and lifestyle that he had introduced to Alex. The last thing he would do was make an excuse for both of them. It was wrong, and it had to be fixed. He had to make things right.

Max needed time to think everything through. There was no room for mistakes. Mistakes cost lives, reputations, and relationships. Knowing full well that his one mistake had cost him his son and Alex's love caused him to be careful.

After thinking all night, he decided to text and send Alex e-mails until she responded. Lying on the bed with his feet crossed and no sign of sleep, he sent off another round of text messages.

Max: Alex, my love, when will u allow me to see you and feel ur warm body? I can't sleep, I can't eat. I'm dying.

He sent it, and minutes later, a text came from Alex to Max's surprise.

Alex: Mr. Blackstone, if u think that I will feel anything about u and for u but contempt then u don't know what u have done to my life by just knowing u. I will never have anything to do with u.

Max: Alex, how can u say such hurtful things? I told u how much I love u and how much u mean to me.

Alex: I can't trust anything u say and I refuse to let my son see u.

Max: He's our son, Alex, and let me be clear, u will never keep me from my son.

Alex: Let me be clear, Max. If u try to find him, u can't and I will have the courts on my side because u are mixed up in a murder case.

Max: I explained all of that to u.

Alex: Not to my satisfaction.

Max: Alex, then allow me to see u one more time. I can't stand for u to be so cold. Alex: Yes, Max, especially since u have had a diet of sex. I guess u can't wean urself off of ur head between my legs just like that, so I'm going to do it for u. I have met someone and I'm going to see where it leads me. I may have him adopt Maxim.

Max: Then u leave me no alternative but to obtain custody of my son.

Alex: That sounds like a threat, Max.

Max: Absolutely!

Max sat stunned, staring at the wall. He didn't move, he didn't beg Alex, and he did not want to fight her, so she left him no choice.

Alex sat up and waited for Max's text. She had shot an arrow into the air and waited for it to come down, but it didn't. It did not come down all that night and it did not come down all that day.

Maybe she'd hit the target. She didn't want to hit the target; she just wanted to get Max's attention. "You can't treat me this way and expect me not to respond," she said to the phone. He hadn't explained anything to her. She was forced to do this, she rationalized.

The only thing Alex had accomplished was to piss off Max, because he called his lawyers and proceeded to make arrangements to see his son and gain custody. He felt that she didn't want to have anything to do with him. She had stated her feelings casually as if he meant nothing to her.

He would prevent her from disappearing with his son while leaving a trail of his broken heart, lust, and love behind her. He would fix the problem, even if he had to destroy their love and then build it back again.

Chapter 8

"Alex, it took weeks to find you. Why haven't you contacted your parents?" Joshua scolded Alex. "You left the apartment, which was not a bad idea, but here you are living in this hovel alone. You never liked to live alone, and in this dump," Joshua said, walking around and trailing his hand on the back of a Victorian couch, where there were two holes in the seating cushions. He sat down, and his body sank lower as if he had fallen into a sinkhole.

"I've been depressed. You do a lot of things when you grow up. I'm here until I can get a better job, or some money that can take me back to New York where I can get a good job and disappear with my son."

"Your parents contacted me because the address you gave them didn't work. They sent mail and it was returned. They tried sending you a text and e-mail, but you never responded."

"I was busy interviewing for jobs and my phone was off. Just when I thought I was going to be hired, I was never called back. Max, that fucking Black... blackballed me. He has prevented me from getting money to take care of myself and my son. He wants me to come crawling back to him. *Fuck him.* I refuse to; I refuse to let any man control me." Alex shifted in her seat, shaking one crossed leg. Josh scanned her body, and he feared for her.

"Well, I hate to tell you, but he has petitioned the courts for his son."

"He did what? He's trying to hurt me, Joshua." Alex sank beside him with her head lowered, and she placed one hand to the back of her neck and rubbed it.

"I guess, like you hurt him. You told him that someone was going to adopt his son. You don't threaten a man like him."

"He told you that?"

"Where would I get that from? You said it, didn't you?"

"What was I to do? There was a young woman found dead in his apartment, for Christ's sake. He didn't want to explain, and he didn't. He just said that his lawyer will take care of it. Then he had the nerve to ask me to make love to him. I'm done with him. I'm so done."

"Look, Alex, you're upset, and I don't want to know about your love life. That's none of my business. This is what I'm going to do," Joshua said, smiling and taking her hand. "I'm going to get you an apartment under my name in Seattle and pay for your flight to Seattle where you can be with your son. Then maybe the judge will rule in your favor."

"Are you saying that I have a chance to prevent Max from gaining control of my son?"

"A small one, but a chance. He's a powerful man. Get ready. You can be on a flight tonight. I have a flight booked leaving at midnight."

Alex ran to Joshua and looped her hands around his neck, kissing him on his cheek.

"I don't know what to say, Joshua."

"Tell me 'thank you' and get your ass on the next plane. Your apartment will be waiting for you. I'll lend you some money to take care of your son until you and Max sort everything out."

"There is no me and Max."

"Don't be so sure, Alex. Max is not a bad fellow, but that twin of his—that's another issue."

"Don't go all soft on me, Josh. You were the one that said he was shady." Alex gazed at Joshua with her wide eyes, waiting for a response.

"That was before I realized that you loved him, and I could never have you the way I want."

"You will always have me, Josh."

"I know, but not the way I want." He repeated his statement, and Alex knew what he meant. There was no need to say any more.

"Go pack." Joshua pushed Alex through the bedroom door as he sat waiting for her in the small living room. Looking around, he said, "What are you doing with all this junk?"

"Oh... they're not mine." Alex stood with a towel barely covering her full breasts. Josh tried to turn away, but the sight of her alluring breasts grabbed him, and he nervously fiddled with his hands. "I rented this apartment fully furnished in case Max came snooping around looking for me when I was Rebecca. I finally found a use for it since the rent was paid up for a year."

Joshua thought that he had never seen Alex look more beautiful. Her tousled hair framed her face, falling aimlessly and covering her breasts. She smiled, and he could not remember the last time she smiled. He gave her a faint smile and waved at her. "Go... go take your shower."

Alex disappeared into the shower. The hot water appeared to wash away her cares. She decided that she would not think about Max, and she would not worry about tomorrow because she had to make it through this day. Every time she thought about him she found it hard to commit to removing him from her life.

⚊⚊⚊◉⚊⚊⚊

JOSHUA ACCOMPANIED Alex on the plane to Seattle. When they arrived at the Seattle airport from San Francisco, he had a car waiting.

"This is impressive, Joshua."

"I'm doing great at Blackstone Enterprises. Pretty soon I'll get the position of general manager of all of Max's hotels in the Americas, and soon the world, then you can marry me." Joshua threw that out. He didn't expect an answer, and by Alex's expression, she didn't even hear him.

Alex shifted in her seat and looked at Joshua. "You are ambitious, and I'm seeing you for the first time. You're on a first-name basis with Max?"

"Well, he asked me to call him Max. We are thick as thieves. I scratch his back, give him some bogus information on you, and he promotes me. One hand washes another."

"Did it occur to you that he was using you?"

"I think we had this conversation before. I'm using him as well."

"But you're not the same as him. He can be ruthless. You don't get to be a billionaire and not leave bodies on the floor. I mean literally."

Joshua reached for a bottle of water and opened it and drank some. "This is good. I've never had water like this." Alex glanced at Joshua and shook her head. "What? What was that about?" Joshua said.

"I can't believe how you've changed." You don't know who you're dealing with. I have trusted you with my life and my son's and here you are accepting gifts from Max."

"These aren't gifts. I've worked hard for this."

"The only thing you've worked hard at is selling me out. Where are your three pieces of silver?"

"There it is, you ungrateful minx." Joshua pointed at the building lit up with lights.

Looking up at the expensive ultramodern apartment—a glass and steel structure with LED lights providing a glow over all of the building—Alex's mouth opened wide.

"It's nice, Joshua. It's very nice."

"It's better than that. It is fucking awesome," he said with wide, beaming eyes.

"I can't live here with you, because Max will find out."

"You can for now."

"But only for a few weeks until I locate an apartment that I can afford," Alex admitted.

"You can't afford anything now. I can give you more money. I have more than I need. I'm just a simple cowboy from Montana."

"Not anymore. I've never seen anyone take to high living in such a short period of time as you."

"You shame me, Alex."

"Well, you ought to be ashamed of yourself." The driver stopped and opened the door, then took Alex's luggage out of the car.

"I'll walk you to the apartment and then I'm out of here. I have a room at the hotel, and you should see it. Max has an opening next week, but he'll be here in Seattle tomorrow." Joshua rocked with excitement as he reached for Alex's hand, helping her navigate the curb.

"He's going to be here tomorrow?" Alex said with a quiver in her voice. She couldn't stand to be in the same city as Max. Their connection was too strong, and every time she tried to distance herself, something drew her in, and she found herself edging closer to him. She'd left Montana to forget him and found she was pregnant. The pregnancy and the birth of her son brought her to San Francisco, where she could be close to Maxim and Max. Now she was in Seattle and once again he had showed up. *Is there any place that I can run to where he won't find me?* she thought.

"I'm afraid so, but it's only for an hour. Then he has to fly out."

"Where is he going?" she questioned, trying to disguise the concern and jealousy that had stirred in her, because she missed the warmth of his deliciously sexy body. She couldn't shower without thinking about how he made love to her in the most sexual and private ways. She could not bathe without touching herself, hoping to simulate the way he placed his fingers on her clit and brought her to the most intense orgasms.

Alex hadn't had sexual release since the last time she laid eyes on her beautiful, profound, exasperating, and sexy man. She felt dead without having his warm dick to enter her body. She missed the excitement of him, his spanking, and his oral sex. *What if he cannot resist the temptations of other women giving him what he needs?* she thought.

Her temptation was Maximilian Blackstone.

"He's celebrating the opening of a new casino hotel in China with his partners here in Seattle."

"Can I come to the opening with you, Josh?" Josh looked speculatively at Alex.

"I... I don't know. You could get me in a lot of trouble." Joshua thought about it for a few minutes. "Yes, what the hell. It could be a good career move," he said, shaking his head. "Max may want to give me that position in China just to get me out of the picture." A sly smile crossed Joshua's mouth, and his eyes moved rapidly as if he were planning his next steps.

"For just a simple cowboy, you appear to have taken to the easy life pretty damn fast."

"Well, you know how it is, money and power corrupt."

"And you don't have enough of both to corrupt anything or anyone, especially me."

"You are one of those rare women who wants love and to hell with money." His finger tipped his expensive aviator glasses forward. Looking over them, he said, "That is, until you need both, then let's see what you'll do. As I remember, that's how I met you at Blackstone's ski lodge."

"All right, Josh, you don't have to be nasty. It doesn't become you."

"It comes with the job." And he flashed a bright, new wicked smile. "How am I doing? Do I remind you of someone?"

"Yes, and it's scary."

Chapter 9

Finding a small bungalow with what Alex could afford wasn't easy. When she did, she moved out of Joshua's apartment before Max got wind of it.

A persuasive knock shook her door, and Alex scooted to it, peeping reluctantly through the small rectangle, filled with Tiffany glass. "Who is it?"

"Detective Blake Scotto. Please, open the door."

He heard the sound of a latch and then the door swung wide. Alex stood in shorts frayed on each leg and a halter top. She appeared much younger than her twenty-three years. Blake thought that she was hotter than he could imagine any woman he had set eyes on. "I have a bell," she said, annoyed, pointing to it. "What brings you her, Detective Scotto?" Alex leaned on the wood frame with her legs crossed. She remembered thinking that if he could find her, then so could Max.

"It's out of habit. Please, call me Blake. I'm here on a personal call. I'm here to warn you that we don't have anyone in custody for that heiress's murder."

"It was murder?" Alex's blue eyes opened wide, and her voice was shrill.

"We're not quite sure... it's still under investigation." Blake stood at the door, then asked, "Can I come in, Ms. Bishop?"

Alex did not say a word; just the gesture of moving away from the door was the invite. He walked in and looked around. "Please, sit... Blake." His eyes darted around the room. It was the nature of his job. He didn't know how to be anything but a policeman. He had joined the police force after three tours in Afghanistan. He had been a policeman at twenty-five, but in his heart, he had been a cop since he could remember. All he'd ever wanted to do was prevent bad things from happening to people, but he found that was impossible, so he settled for the next best thing and that was catching the bad guys.

He'd wanted nothing more until he felt his heart hitch when he met Alex. Alex's glance covered Blake. His face handsome and rawboned, with a strong jaw and piercing deep-blue eyes. His clothes were casual—his brown slacks fell on his hips and his long-sleeve shirt, rolled at the wrists, revealed muscles in his taut arms. He wore an inexpensive Swiss watch with a leather band, but his shoes were expensive. His shoes indicated that he respected his feet and probably the time he spent on them.

"Detective Scotto…" Alex caught herself, "Blake… you didn't tell me why you're here."

"I was wondering whether you would like to go to dinner with me."

"You didn't come to Seattle to ask me out to dinner, did you?" A small, easy smile crossed her face.

"As a matter of fact, I did."

"I don't know what to say. Is that allowed?" Alex queried. "I mean… to date someone that's involved in one of your cases?"

"You're not a suspect in that case. There is only one person of interest…"

"And that is?" Alex's and Blake's eyes locked.

"It's Maximilian Blackstone. It won't be long before we know how the girl died." Alex's heart sank and her pulse raced.

"Did you come here to get more information on Max? Because…"

"No. I came here to see you." Silence passed between Blake and Alex.

She felt as if she was being unfaithful to Max. The intensity of Blake's eyes was compelling, as if he could make love to her with his eyes. She felt uneasy, and her heart fluttered and screamed, *Take me away, Max. Take me away from this man, because you are in jeopardy of losing me.*

Alex rose and said, "Give me a few minutes and I'll get dressed and meet you on the Wharf."

"Do you know Andres? It's a wonderful seafood place where we can talk."

"Yes, I know exactly where it is. This is my home. I was born in Seattle," Alex added.

"So was I. That's amazing."

Blake rose from the couch and stood. Walking to the door, he paused a moment and leaned in to kiss Alex, but she pulled away. He understood. Maybe it was too early to try to kiss her. Maybe she didn't like him that way. *Maybe I'm not rich enough*, he thought. But how could it be? It was Alex who had left Blackstone, who could buy and sell him a thousand times over.

He had to take it slow. Walking to his car he, noticed a car parked a few houses away. Why was someone watching Alex's house? It came to Blake immediately that it had to be Blackstone.

⬗

"MAX, SHE INVITED THAT detective in, and he stayed there for an hour." It was a mere fifteen minutes, but Jonas was prone to exaggeration.

"He could be questioning her," Max said casually, trying not to reveal how his heart ached for Alex, and how he had to prevent himself from rushing to her house, which would put him in a bad position in family court.

"Look, Jonas, I have to speak to my lawyers. I have to be in court tomorrow. Call me in twenty minutes." He could not concentrate because of Jonas's meddling.

Jonas's constant interference had taken on a life of its own. The first girl Max fell in love with in high school, Jonas followed her around to prove that she would sleep with anyone. His rationale was that if she really liked Max, then she would never have gone to bed with him.

What he neglected to tell the girl was that he was Max's twin. His explanation was that she should have known the difference.

When he could no longer persuade Max to give her up, he set her up with a date, and when she accepted, he hired a private detective to get pictures and sent them to Max. It had been three years since Max had heard from or about Gale. Then on the day that he discovered that Alex and Rebecca were the same person, she was found strangled in his apartment.

Until he resolved the problem of Gale's murder, there would be no rest for Max. Now he had to contend with a man vying for Alex's affection. Max would have Detective Scotto investigated, and then he would know whether there would be a problem with him.

He called his security personnel in San Francisco. "Do whatever it takes to find out about Scotto. And use the same methods as usual—keep everything from Jonas."

———— ◉ ————

BLAKE WATCHED IN AWE as Alex strutted through the doors of the restaurant and their eyes met. She pointed, and the young maître d' led her to Blake's table. He stood, and the maître d' pulled out her chair. "So formal. Please, sit, Blake."

"I was only acknowledging that a beautiful woman had entered the room."

"Thank you." A server placed water at the table, and a waiter standing nearby asked for their drink order. "I seldom drink liquor," Alex said, "I'll have..."

"Please, have a glass of wine. You do drink wine?" Blake questioned.

"Well, just this time. I'll have..."

"What is it?"

"I was going to order a very expensive wine out of habit," Alex said with a smile.

"Do you think I couldn't afford it?"

"It's not that..." she said, apologizing for what she thought was an insensitive and rude statement on her part.

"Well, you are correct. I probably couldn't afford it." They looked at each other, and they both laughed. "I know I can't compete with Blackstone, but I'm willing to try. I can barely afford to bring you here, but I can do it maybe once a month, if you don't mind?"

"I like your honesty and straightforwardness," Alex said, glancing warmly at Blake.

"Tell me, Alex, how did you meet Blackstone?"

"That's very private and very personal." Alex lowered her eyes and turned her head away from Blake.

"You are direct. I guess I have overstepped my bounds."

"Please, understand that I'm in love with Max. I don't want to encourage you. If you want to see me as a friend, then that's all I can give for now. We have a son together and he may try to take him, and I can't allow him to use anything against me."

"I understand."

Blake's and Alex's eyes met. "I'm sorry, Alex, enough with the questions. I've been a policeman so long that I don't know how to be with a woman without interrogating her. I see you need to relax, and I need the time off."

"Maybe you need to be on the hot seat." She eyed Blake, raising one eyebrow. "So, what made you leave Seattle for San Francisco?"

His eyes lowered as if searching for an answer, and a long pause ensued. Then he raised his head. "I arrived home from the army and found that my sister had disappeared. I searched for her, and then I joined the police department. I came across some leads but never was able to locate her. The department that I was working in promoted me to detective and then let me go, because the case consumed all my time; it had gotten too personal. The department in San Francisco decided to take a chance on me, and I was able to spend my time searching for my sister and working on my cases."

Alex listened and watched Blake's eyes; there was honesty and caring when he spoke of his sister. She was never able to read Max. He was a ball of confusion. One minute he appeared to be troubled and the next he was a carefree sexual animal. It was when he spoke of their son that she recognized the honesty and caring she had not seen in his face before. It was as if he had secrets, and this troubled her.

Her life was a fairy tale when she first met Max, but now it was fractured. Now she had to live in the real world and become the person her parents had hoped she would be.

Blake was the first chance she had to show her parents that she was no longer a child and accept her working-class roots. *My father would like Blake*, she thought.

He reached across and placed his not-so-manicured hand over hers. It was not the hand of a man who received manicures every day; it was the hand of a man who had a tough life. His knuckles were scarred, and an old wound ran across both hands. The wounds were deep.

"I see you looking at my hands. Well, this occurred—" he said, pointing at the wound. "—when arresting a fugitive and I tried to talk him out of killing his wife. He turned the knife on me, but the woman was safe. And no, I didn't shoot him. It's all part of the job." Blake saw an expression of relief cross Alex's face.

"I would be terrified if I had a man who risks his life each time he leaves the house."

"If you were mine, I would get into another line of business."

"You're making me uncomfortable," Alex said, reaching for her glass of wine.

"That's not my intention. My intention is to tell you that I plan on making you my girl." He reached for her hand and placed his on top of it. She didn't flinch or pull it from under his. Blake captured her gaze, but from the corner of Alex's eye, she spied a figure.

There was a silhouette of a tall man in the dimly lit restaurant gliding in her direction. His stride was long to fit the long legs that strutted across the floor. His face was pensive, and his brow knitted as he headed closer. Alex soon recognized the figure, and a sigh of excitement and panic crossed her lips.

Max stalked in their direction. His gorgeous face with a short, manicured beard, deep dimples, and sea-green eyes made Alex hot for him, and she crossed her legs tightly to keep from shaking. She felt Blake could feel her nervousness and Max would tune into her sexual heat any minute. It was impossible, but nevertheless, she wasn't taking any chances. He wore an off-white V-neck silk sweater and black pants. He had on black loafers, and he looked smoking hot.

"No, it can't be," she said. Her hand trembled under Blake's, and she pulled it to her lap.

"What is it, Alex?'

"It's Black. I mean Max."

"Blackstone. What is he doing here?"

"He came for me." She turned in her chair to face Max, and his gaze locked on her, then he focused his eyes on Blake.

Max strode up to their table. "Alex, what are you doing with that detective?"

"She's having dinner with me."

"I did not ask you, Detective Scotto. I asked my fiancée. She can speak for herself."

Blake rose from his chair and met Max eye to eye. Alex rose and stood in between them.

"Please, don't make a scene, Max. I have a right to see whomever I want whenever I want, because I'm no longer your fiancée, remember? I sent you back your ring and necklace and all your little playthings."

"Not all of them," Max quipped with a wry smile and a twist of his head. "We have a child together, and you are out with this person whom I have yet to investigate fully."

"The only person that needs investigating is you, Mr. Blackstone, and I will do my best to find out what you're hiding."

"Call me Max. I'm sure you have a few skeletons that would interest your department, and besides, I can recognize a fox when I see one," Max stated with a wrinkled brow, his dimples digging into his chiseled face each time he spoke.

"And I can recognize a wolf," Blake retorted, tightening his jaw. "You are interrupting my dinner and I'm going to see if someone can have you removed from the premises." Blake took a step past Max.

"It would take a court order, because I own the place," Max said, straightening his head and planting his feet in a wide stance.

"Let's go, Blake. We can get a hamburger. I wasn't born with a silver spoon in my mouth," Alex said, her eyes cutting through Max's heart as she picked up her small purse and headed for the exit with Blake bounding after her. Max watched as she walked out of his life once more.

Max reeled around and his long legs strode across the floor. He reached Alex at the doorway. Blake stepped aside to open the door. Max softly touched her elbow. She turned, knowing the touch. "Talk to me, Alex."

"We have nothing to say to each other."

Blake stood waiting.

Max leaned in to kiss her, and she moved away. "You don't want my kisses?"

"I don't need them. There is a difference." She walked away from Max.

When they reached the second door, Blake held it open, and Alex stepped outside. He turned and sent Max a long stare.

"Blake... Blake, our evening is ruined. I don't feel like eating or anything."

"That's exactly what Blackstone wanted," Blake said, clutching her hand.

"You're right. He's probably celebrating with a drink and having both of us followed and you investigated right at this moment. My car is in the parking lot." She looped her arm under his and they strolled uneasily to her banged-up yellow-and-black convertible Volkswagen Beetle.

"This is yours?"

"Yes, do you have a problem with it?" A peal of laughter rang from both.

"I thought you would be driving a Mercedes. I was told—"

"But did they tell you that I returned everything to Max, including the engagement ring."

"I think someone did mention that, but I didn't believe him."

"Tell your partner that there are some people in the world that do not define themselves by how many things they accumulate. I never wanted anything from him. I have all I need now."

"Your son," Blake interrupted.

"Yes, my beautiful son, Maxim. Blake, this will never work out. Max will never give us a moment of peace," Alex said, facing reality.

"I'm used to living on the edge. I can handle him."

"I said before that I love him. I don't want you to handle him. I can't see you, or anyone else, until we resolve our problems." Alex placed her hand to Blake's face, "You don't understand. A man like him will never give me up, even if he doesn't want me. I'm like a trophy he hangs on the wall, where he can look at it and show it off to his friends, or keep for his own amusement."

"No, you're wrong. You're his everything. I can see that in his eyes. If you were mine, you would be cherished."

"I'm my own person, and don't you forget it, Detective Scotto." Alex placed a kiss on his cheek.

Alex stepped into the Volkswagen and held the wheel as Blake closed the door. She hit a switch and her window slid down.

"I'm going to follow you home to make sure you're safe," he said.

"No, don't do that. I'm in a custody battle with Max for my son. I don't need him bringing up anything concerning another man."

"Does that mean that you won't see me?"

"No, it doesn't mean that. It means that I won't see you until this matter is over between me and Max." Alex glanced up at Blake and saw disappointment in his eyes, and she fastened her seat belt and drove off. She couldn't handle any more possessive and domineering men. Her mind was full of the lack of money and a battle with a man that could buy her and sell her many times over. *I must be a fool to think that I can fight Max in court. But I have to try.* Alex talked to herself the next ten miles home.

Chapter 10

Arriving home earlier than she anticipated, Alex decided to update her résumé and send out a few applications online. She had joined LinkedIn but then decided against it. She didn't want him to have a paper trail on her. An e-mail came in, and she looked and saw it was from Blackstone's company. *There is nothing wrong with opening it*, she thought.

Alex,

I'm sorry. Can you forgive me? I can't sleep without you. You're making me crazy.

Max

She was excited that he had e-mailed her. She didn't want to have to worry about whom he was thinking about. She knew his sexual appetite; it was enormous.

Mr. Blackstone,

You have embarrassed me. What are you going to do next?

Alex

Alex,

I wouldn't do anything to hurt my beautiful, sexy girl. I need you tonight.

Max

Can I trust him? she questioned. She needed to be with him and know that he loved her and that he wouldn't take their son if she didn't agree with him. She needed to know that he still desired her, and most of all, she needed to be in his arms and feel him inside of her.

Alex,

I'm waiting for your answer. We will discuss our son.

Max

Max,

I'll see you, but for only an hour. Then you have to leave.

Alex

I'll be there in a minute.

Max

Alex walked to the restroom to freshen up when the bell rang. How could it be Max that soon? He must have been sitting in his limo e-mailing her. She scampered to the door and, not bothering to look through the peephole, she opened the door wide.

"Blake, you shouldn't be here. Max is coming over."

"I wanted to make sure you were safe. I didn't see a light, and—"

"He will be over any minute and it will not look good for me if you are leaving my house."

"I'm leaving now. Don't trust him, Alex. There is still a dead woman—"

"Please, go now." And she pushed him out of the door and closed it.

Blake stood on the porch for a few minutes until he saw Max's limo cruise up and stop at the small bungalow. He walked past the car, turning he spied Max exit the car and look in his direction. Blake got the reaction he wanted. He could see the anger in Max's face.

Max raised his finger and rang the bell. Alex opened the door and met Max's gaze. "Come in." A silent Max entered and looked around. Alex crossed her arms and turned her back. He followed her through the foyer and to the living area. The house was furnished in '50s decor. There was an old, worn brown couch, and two giant wooden lamps with white shades covering the bulbs bracketed it. Alex saw Max's face. "I know, but this is the best I can do. I just got a job at a restaurant. I sent my résumé out all over town and I haven't heard from anyone else yet. But I know I will get a call very soon."

"Are you planning on raising my son in an environment like this, Alex?" Max's brow furrowed, and lines of anger deepened his face.

"It's all I can afford. My parents are going to help me, and when I have to work they will babysit. He's staying with them until I can get his room together."

"And when will that be? I can pay for everything you need. Arrange for better living conditions. Move you into my penthouse, build you a house, or if you prefer, you and my boy can have my home in Montana."

"I don't know. All I need is my son and you're threatening to separate us."

"You have been separated from him for a year."

"I was busy concentrating on his father, hoping that I could make you see me as I am, and not the sex-hungry slut you seem to be attracted to."

"I want you and my son. I don't want just him. Can't you see, Alex?" His brow smoothed and his eyes softened. He stepped closer to her, and her resolve weakened. They stared long at each other, but the stillness was broken when Max reached for Alex with both hands and held her face. He leaned close, his lips met hers, and his tongue entered with ease as if it was made for her mouth.

The kiss was wet and hot. His lips covered her mouth. Pushing her against the wall with his hands and his hard body, Max sank to his knees, and he began lifting her skirt. Then anxiously he ripped her skirt off and threw it to the floor. She watched his head move as he placed kisses on her stomach. His hands were under her bra, and he lifted it over her breasts. Her nipples stood hard and erect.

His fingers caressed her nipples. Max eased his hands between her legs and pulled her thong to the side. His mouth cupped her mound. His tongue found her clit. And his fingers pried open her folds. His moaning became louder and louder. "I need this," he said, glancing up at her. "Tell me you will never allow another man to kiss you like this." As he begged Alex, he pulled her thong down, and she stepped out of it.

Alex's head fell back, and she quietly moaned, "No one will ever have me but you. Don't stop, Max... don't stop loving me."

She felt his curly locks and weaved her hands through his hair, and with a fistful of hair, she pulled hard as he buried his head deep into her mound. His tongue measured each vibration of her clit, knowing that she was on the verge of an orgasm. He intermittently glanced up at her face, knowing that she was in the throes of a long-awaited orgasm.

Alex's head leaned far back against the wall, and she shouted, "Max, I'm coming." She finally admitted that she was in the sub position when she asked his permission to have her orgasm. He was that strong a force in her sexual life. Max knew now that Alex had become what he wanted, and his need to dominate her was finally realized.

"You may come," Max said, gazing up at the tortured look on Alex's face. And then there was a calm that washed over her like the eye of a hurricane.

"I want you to come once more." And he buried his face deep beneath her legs and placed one finger in her vagina and one in her anus with his tongue on her clit.

"This is wonderful. I'm coming again," she admitted. Max pulled his finger out of her anus and circled the rim of her anus and a convulsion of orgasms occurred.

With her back to the wall, Alex gasped for breath. Her knees wobbled, and Max caught her in his arms, lifted her, and brought her to the bed. He laid her down, and he disrobed. "Alex, turn on your stomach." Alex followed his directions. She lay still as Max massaged her back. Her eyes closed as his hands rubbed the nape of her neck and down to her back, and then with both hands he massaged her buttocks. She could not remember when she last felt so serene. She had wanted this day to come, and she fell under his spell once more.

He leaned forward and trailed his mouth down her back to her buttocks. He nipped each buttock one at a time. A moment of silence occurred. "What is it, Max?"

"I can't do this."

"What do you mean?" *What the fuck is he talking about? Is he doing this to fuck with my head?*

"I'm not seeing you as my sexual partner. I'm seeing you as the mother of my child."

"And what does that mean?" *I thought that this was what he wanted. Now I know what he is looking for. He wants someone like Rebecca—no ties and no children.*

"It means that I can't satisfy my sexual fantasies with you any longer."

Then with whom are you going to fuck, suck, and paddle? What the fuck am I thinking? Better yet, what am I doing?

Alex sat up in bed, resting on the wrought-iron headboard. "You must be kidding me, Max. You introduced me to this lifestyle of yours and I accepted everything about it, and now you tell me that because I have your child we can no longer make love to each other the way you have indoctrinated me."

"No. I... I'm unable to be turned on the way I once was by you."

"What does that mean for our relationship? What does this mean for us?" A long silence passed between them. Alex could not believe that she had run away from him only to allow him to get close to her and reject her. Her body ached with the want of his body next to her and the pleasure they'd had between them—the spankings and oral sex that went on and on day and night. Was he that sick that he couldn't have sex with her unless she was that sexy Dominatrix, Rebecca? Well, Alex decided that she would not play his games anymore, not another day.

"I'm not sure, Alex. I have to leave." Alex watched as Max dressed in silence, then he leaned in to kiss her, and she pulled away. Her handsome lover, whom she had been satisfying and longing for, didn't find her appealing.

How fucked up can this be? she thought. *Where is Joshua when I need him?*

"WHAT BRINGS YOU IN so soon, Mr. Blackstone?"

"I'm having problems functioning sexually."

"On your last visit you appeared to have a sexual life to be envied. You had a problem sleeping, but you have that under control. What is going on now?"

"The woman I'm in love with and the mother of my child..."

"Did you say she had a child for you? You never mentioned that."

"Yes. I found out about a month ago."

"That could be your problem. A man becomes a father and suddenly his whole world is topsy-turvy. He's responsible for a young life, and giving attention to his wife or significant other and his job. These are demanding," the therapist said with a sigh.

Max raised his head. "I'm in a custody battle with my... my significant other. I find her sexually breathtaking when I'm pleasing her, but when it's time to engage in my sexual pursuits, I freeze."

The therapist wrote some notes and turned to face Max. "Mr. Blackstone, you have communicated with me concerning your sexual proclivities in the past, and I have advised you. This is perhaps a more difficult situation to diagnose because it is cognitive. You may need a psychologist instead of a sex therapist. I can refer you to one if you would like. For now, Mr. Blackstone, you may need some time away from Ms. Bishop and then see what happens. I suggest writing your thoughts in a diary, not every day, but when you are under extreme sexual or mental pressure."

Max sucked in a deep breath and exhaled. "Thank you. If I find in the future that I can't handle this situation, then I'll ask for a referral." Max shook the therapist's hand and left. As he walked through the glass corridor, his smartphone rang.

"What is it, Jonas?" Max said irritated.

"Well, what did that quack say?"

"None of your business."

"Are you still having problems sleeping? Or is it your girl again? Man, a woman with a body like that… I would fuck her day and night."

"Shut up, Jonas. You're not making this any easier. She's the mother of my child."

"Do you hear yourself? What is wrong with you? I've never seen you act nuts behind a woman before. I bet I know why you're at that quack's office…"

"I'm not interested, Jonas. Listen, I will be in Las Vegas this afternoon. Try not to get in any trouble. See you tomorrow in San Francisco."

———◆———

JONAS CALLED SOPHIA in Las Vegas. "Hi, are you busy this afternoon?"

"I have one client, but I can cancel for you."

"It's not me, darling. It's Max. He may need you. He's all uptight over his woman and child. She's giving him a hard time. He's crazy about her."

"But what can I do?"

"You know what he likes and needs. I don't think he's getting what you specialize in. You know, the bondage and whippings. He's a powerful man, and he has to be in control. When this does not occur, it's because that woman is not being submissive enough. I need you to role-play with him. Let him control you and punish you."

"You know this will cost you, and you owe me, Jonas."

"Just go to his room. He should be arriving in about an hour. The concierge will let you into his penthouse. I'll call and inform him that you will be there."

Jonas called and tried to contact Max to let him know that Sophia would be there to service him, but he didn't get an answer. After the call, Jonas went about being Jonas—spoiled, devious, pretending he was Maximilian Blackstone.

MAX OPENED THE RECLINER and lay back. He raised a glass of red wine, took a whiff, and looked at it, and then took a large gulp. His Learjet would land in an hour. Feeling lonely, he needed Alex more than he could imagine. He wanted his son, and he wanted Alex. Nothing else mattered in the scheme of things. Not money or power, not even sex. He wanted a family, and they could work the rest out later. There was too much running around in his head for him to concentrate on sex.

He surprised himself when he picked up his smartphone to call Alex. "Alex, I'm sorry. Can you forgive me? I don't know what happened. That never happened before." Alex didn't know how to respond. She was tired of the roller-coaster ride she found herself on with Max. First he left her when she first met him with no explanation, then a brother, then his sexual antics and a dead heiress, and now he could not respond to her sexually.

"I know what the problem is, Max. Yes, I forgive you. We have been so preoccupied with fighting over our son that we are losing each other. You're a special man who happens to have unusual sexual habits. I can't expect you to change overnight, and that is what you're trying to do to please me. I don't want anyone but you, and I know that I will have to give you what you need."

"Baby, I'll send a jet for you. Come to me and marry me, will you? I want a family. I want you." When Max called Alex "baby," she melted. He sounded vulnerable. It was the first time he had called her that. She would not dwell on whether he had said that before to another woman. Now was not the time. She wanted him any way she could have him.

"I'll be ready in fifteen minutes. And yes, I'll marry you. My son needs a father and I need you."

"I'll send a car to meet the jet in Vegas. Don't buy any clothes; we can go shopping. You can buy whatever you desire. You have made me the happiest man in the world."

———◦———

MAX ARRIVED AT BLACKSTONE Casino Hotel in Las Vegas half an hour early with no turbulence and no delays because of weather. He was walking on air when he settled into his penthouse suite. He rushed into the shower because he wanted to be ready for Alex. Knowing that his life was about to change, he welcomed the changes. Now he would have a family, his son, Alex, and her parents. Oh, but what should he do about Jonas?

Sophia had arrived early and prepared herself for a workday. She showered in one of the bedrooms and dressed in knee-high black boots and a short, patent-leather dress with slits on two sides. Under the dress she wore nothing but a shaved mound. Hearing the shower, she casually walked out of the room and met Max in his bedroom.

"What are you doing here, Sophia?" Max said, loud with surprise.

"Why, I heard that you needed my services."

"I haven't needed you—"

"Since you met Rebecca. I know."

"You can't be here, Sophia. I'm expecting my fiancée at any time, and we're to be married."

"Congrats, then my services aren't needed? Just wait until I see that brother of yours."

"I will never need them again." Max threw on a white robe that read blackstone and hurried Sophia to the elevator door. He grabbed his trench coat and draped it over her shoulders as he reached for his wallet, which lay in a crystal bowl. He placed a wad of hundred-dollar bills in her hand. "I hope that's enough. Please go."

She looked at Max and replied, "Jonas usually takes care of me." The elevator opened on Max standing with his robe open and a terrified look in his eyes, and Sophia clutching money in her hands. She clicked the black stiletto boots and flashed a smile at Alex.

"Is this how you plan on spending our honeymoon night? Are you trying to get help so you can fuck me? Is this the kind of life you are going to live with me and my son?"

Max stood still and could not speak. Sophia didn't know what to do except walk between the two lovers.

"I'm sorry," Sophia apologized. "I'm just doing my job." She eyed Alex as if to say, *Now you do yours.*

"Wait, don't go anywhere, you." Alex reached into her purse, and her hand clutched her phone. She took it out and before Max could say "wait," she took a picture of Sophia and him.

"The judge should be interested in these pictures." Sophia left without Max and Alex noticing because their eyes were focused on each other.

"It's not what you think, Alex. I—"

"You planned on getting in a little BDSM before you married me. I would have to spend my days worrying about why you never wanted to fuck me."

"Listen to yourself, Alex. That's not you."

"I don't know who I am anymore. Were you making love to me or Rebecca?"

"Not her again." Max found the nearest chair and fell into it.

"What do you mean? Are you telling me that you never enjoyed Rebecca sucking your dick and letting you punish her?"

"Why are you talking about yourself in the third person as if you are not that person?"

"I am not that person anymore, and clearly you don't want me unless I'm Rebecca."

"It is you I want to marry, not Rebecca."

"You are marrying me because you want my son."

"I could take our son if I wanted." His eyes were dark and his tone full of arrogance.

"Now you're admitting that you are planning—"

"Can't you see that that's the only way?"

"The only way you will bend me to your will. I've had enough of you and this crazy, fucked-up sexual life. I'm going to find a man that I can have a normal relationship with and—"

"He will never get the opportunity to be with you, because you are mine and I don't let anyone or anything come between what I want and what I need," Max said with a dark hooded expression covering his eyes.

"Are you threatening me, Max?"

Max stood, eyes fixed on Alex as if in a trance. His mind wandering, he realized he could not control Alex. He could not have what he needed in life and wanted so badly. *Maybe she is too young*, he thought. *Maybe she needs time to grow up.* He didn't want to give her that time, or give her up. She might find that she no longer needed him to make her life complete.

Alex didn't wait for an answer. Max gave Alex a hard look, one that made the nape of her neck tremble. One she had never seen before. She wondered what was wrong with him, but she took that opportunity not to find out and rushed to the elevator. Before she could step in, he slid his arm around her waist and another behind her neck.

Max's lips touched hers. It was electric. It jolted her. His tongue snaked into her mouth, and she began sucking it. Her clit became moist, and he slid his hands on both sides of her black pencil skirt, raising it to her waist. His low moan frightened her. The look on his face was that of a predator. He was indeed the wolf that Blake had described in their meeting earlier.

"No. No." She pushed him away. "I can't do this anymore. All we do is fuck and we never solve anything, and you never answer my questions." Max grabbed Alex's hands and led her to the sofa overlooking a panoramic view of the Vegas strip and a mountain range.

"What do you want to know, Alex? Ask," he demanded.

"Start with your brother." He lifted himself and paced around and faced the window.

"Very well." Max exhaled. He took a few moments, trying to fashion a narrative that Alex would understand. "Our parents died when we were five and we inherited millions. I don't know how much. They died in a traffic accident driving to a family meeting, and the last time I remember seeing my mother was when she was in the hospital." My father had died moments before. My mother asked me to take care of Jonas because he was sickly. I have felt burdened by her last wishes all my life because I'm the eldest."

"He's only a few minutes younger than you."

"Yes, but he didn't react well to both our parents dying at the same time. I learned that I had to be strong for both of us; I had to be Jonas's mother and father. After our parents were buried we went to live with our guardians.

"We were not allowed to handle our money until we reached twenty-one. We were treated well by our guardians, but they never showed us love, only that they cared for the money. They had their own children, and we were two boys that were pitied, because we had no family. Our uncles, aunts, and cousins died in a plane crash on their way to the same family hunting event in Montana. Our entire family had been wiped out in two days, and we were orphans. We inherited large sums of money. Some was for our education, and then our guardians used some of the money for living expenses and to educate their children.

"We didn't begrudge the use of the money, because all we wanted to do was be part of their family, which we never were. We were looked on with contempt by our adoptive parents' children because of our wealth. Jonas felt it the most because he was sensitive. He began running away from home, and each time they returned him, his behavior and attitude became worse. He lived on the streets for a while. I spent months looking for him, trying to convince him to come home in the hope that things would be different.

"As we entered our teens, Jonas was running away every week, until one day he didn't come home, and I received a letter informing me that he had enlisted into the army. He had gone to Afghanistan before I had a chance to talk some sense into him. By then I could do nothing for him but pray that he would come home safely.

"When he did return, after serving three tours while I had been safely tucked away in my private college, he came back with a drug addiction and a mental disorder... what is it called?" He snapped his fingers trying to remember.

"PTSD. Post-traumatic Stress Disorder," Alex added, sitting quietly with her hand to her mouth.

"He had been so traumatized and on drugs and alcohol that I had to first send him to drug rehabilitation. When he sobered, he had the nightmares so terrible that I had to sleep at his side to prevent him from hurting himself or someone. I couldn't sleep for weeks no matter how I tried.

"Soon he was able to claim his inheritance and he began spending it on one woman after the next. He spent millions and was soon broke. I had to bankroll him with a business to keep him busy and out of trouble."

"I gather that business is Pandora's Retreat."

"He's just providing a service..."

"For the seriously fucked-up rich," Alex added.

"What do you want from me, Alex? He's my brother and the only family I have except for our son, and for him, I thank you. That business is the only thing that Jonas has excelled at since he was a youth. I love my brother, and I made a promise to my mother to watch over him."

"You can't protect him from himself, Max. You can't be his mother and father and wife. You have a life."

"Not without you, and it would have to include Jonas."

"What would you say if I don't want Jonas in my life and around our son? He is seriously messed up."

"But I can't leave him. Do you understand? Tell me you understand, Alex."

"All I understand is that I can't be in your world anymore, especially since you have not explained the woman that you were engaged to."

"I explained that I broke up our engagement when I first met you in Montana."

"You have said that over and over and yet it does not explain why you are connected to her death."

"You will have to trust me."

"I can't marry you when all you say is, 'I have to trust you.' I have empathy for Jonas, but to tell you the truth, I don't want him around my son."

"Alex, I'm not going to allow you to prevent our son from forming a bond with his only uncle."

"Allow! An uncle that has serious mental problems and may be involved in God knows what."

"He could not do anything to harm another human being. He's too sensitive."

"He saw death in the army, and who knows what else. And what about you, Max? Could you?"

"If that's how you feel, then maybe we should have some time apart."

"No. Not some time—forever. It's over, Max." Standing and looking out on the Vegas strip, Max turned and gazed at Alex. There was a silence, and then he broke it.

"Alex, I want you to know that I have a court order to take our son."

"You bastard." She slapped Max across his face. He wasn't surprised and he didn't move, but when she reached to hit him again, he wrapped his large hand around her wrist, restraining her.

Her eyes blazed. "You got me here under the pretext of marrying me to tell me that you can take my son whenever you want."

"That's not true, Alex. It's not what you think."

"It's exactly what I think. You cannot bend me to your will. It will never happen. I will not sit on my hands while you take my child. How could you do this to me?" Tears welled in her eyes. "How could you do this, Max? I hate you, Max. I will never love you... never."

Max watched as Alex screamed and threw a vase at him. He didn't want that reaction, and clearly something had got out of hand. Their relationship had become toxic. Alex ran for the elevator, and Max didn't stop her.

Chapter 11

A month passed, and Alex couldn't get out of bed. Her court date had come and gone on the hearing for custody of her son. Max called and texted her, but she only stared at the phone, reading the text messages when she felt well enough. He was so use to controlling everything and everyone. First the bondage thing, then a twin brother, and finally taking her son in hopes that he could bend her to his will. She had declared that she hated him and would never love him because of what he had done. It became hard to forgive him.

Alex finally found a job working the evening shift at a hotel as a cocktail waitress. The work paid an above-decent salary. It was one of the best hotels in Seattle, and it was owned by someone that did not require her to submit to the kind of activities that Blackstone had required of her. *Maybe after I save some money, I can hire a real lawyer to fight Max for custody of Maxim*, she thought.

She hadn't seen Maxim in a month because she had to see Max first, and she couldn't bring herself to ask to see her own son. Alex's parents visited Maxim in Montana. Max explained to them that if anyone found out that he was the father, then there was a possibility of a kidnapping. That was why he needed control of their son, to protect him. Alex's mother and father tried to convince Alex to see Max's point. Her father declared that she was stubborn as usual.

Running out of the rented bungalow, late for work, she jumped into her Volkswagen Beetle and gunned the accelerator, thinking she was being tailed. Alex wanted to keep this job a secret. She didn't want anything to interfere with her being able to support herself and her son, and besides, her tips were beginning to add up. She was making five hundred dollars a night and a thousand on Saturdays. Pretty soon she would have enough money to take the great Mr. Blackstone back to court.

Arriving at the St. John Hotel and rushing to the lockers to change into her skimpy black-and-white French maid's uniform with black six-inch heels, she was out of breath. The restaurant in the hotel catered to the very rich. It mirrored Blackstone's Omni hotel, only it didn't have ultramodern furniture. It was more on old-world European model, with its French silk furnishing and original paintings by Monet.

Alex felt lucky to have gotten the job, because the last girl fell in the high heels serving drinks. That was a disaster for her, but a godsend for Alex. "You're late," shouted the pretty waitress with the curvy body. "I'm going to make all those tips if you don't get here on time." Crystal confessed, "If Rob hadn't picked me up, I would be coming in with you now... late." Crystal swung her tray around waiting for the bartender to complete her order.

When Alex had placed an ad in the local newspaper for a roommate, Crystal walked up looking like a member of one of the local rock bands. Her hair was long and black with streaks of red tint, and she wore a short skirt with black-and-white polka dots. She had a fringed vest and boots, straight out of the seventies with a little of the eighties fashion statement.

She swung around carrying a tray with ten drinks. "Which table is mine?" Alex inquired.

"You were requested at that table." Crystal pointed at the table seating ten. Alex peeped around and saw a large party of men dressed immaculately in their Armani suits and ties, with the exception of one man dressed in a gray bespoke suit who had just walked away from the table. She recognized the special tailoring of that suit. It was different. *At a distance it could be one of Black's suits*, Alex thought.

After walking to the table, she asked for their orders. She moved around the rectangular table as each man placed his order. She turned and ran into that bespoke suit, which decorated a handsome gray-blue-eyed man of about forty with salt-and-pepper hair. He was clean-shaven, and his eyes locked on her.

"Aren't you going to take my order?"

"I'm sorry, sir."

"The name is St. John, Ms. Bishop."

"Sir, what would you like?"

"Your telephone number."

"I'm busy now, sir. I don't have time to socialize," she said, meeting his gaze.

"Then just bring me a glass of water," Charles St. John stated with an arresting smile.

"Very well, sir."

Alex gripped the tray to keep from biting her nails. It was as though he had undressed her with his steel-gray eyes. She felt she had seen those eyes before. Every time she brought a drink to his table, his eyes followed her. He sat staring at her as she walked in the high heels. She tried to pull the uniform down, but tore it instead. The heat from his glances went on for hours, and when it was time for her break, he sat in that same position, his fist to his chin, until she returned.

"He's making me nervous," Alex admitted to Crystal. "If I disappear, make sure you tell the police about him."

"He could take me anytime or any day," Crystal said with a chuckle. Alex stood gazing at Crystal thinking, *what a stupid thing to say.*

"I hope you're not that impressionable."

"Why not? I would give anything to land a big fish like him."

"You have my blessings." Alex couldn't get out of her mind the problems she was having with Max, and any man at this time would be nothing but trouble.

"Really?"

"You can even take over my table. Tell them I'm on break."

Alex went to the dressing area and sat to give her feet a rest out of sight of another impossibly handsome man. She couldn't handle one, so how would she navigate around two, both rich and both big trouble?

⸺◉⸺

WHEN ALEX RETURNED from her break, Crystal had taken another drink order.

"I'm glad you're back. I can't keep up with those orders, and those guys are drunk and horny, all except Mr. St. John. I don't trust a man that never takes a drink."

"He likes to be in control," Alex said, glancing at the table.

"How do you know?" Crystal said.

"Trust me. Give me that tray. I'll get the drinks, and you can take a break."

"Don't smile at the one at the end of the table, the one with his back to us, the one all in black. He's mine," Crystal said with a grin.

"Don't worry; I don't have time for any rich, horny men. As a matter of fact, I'm now celibate."

"No shit. How does that feel?"

"It feels damn good." Alex lifted the tray filled with drinks and swung around the corner, strutting with confidence.

"Great, you're back. I was wondering what happened to you," St. John said with his eyes burrowing into her body.

"Here is your water, and a glass of white wine for you, a whiskey soda, a glass of red wine, Scotch, and water." Alex moved around the table looking at the drinks and never looking up. She hadn't noticed the man who had joined the group.

"Ms. Bishop, did you forget me?" It was a familiar voice. It was a sexy voice. It was a domineering voice. Alex glanced across the table, and her eyes locked on the handsome man dressed all in black. He wore a black silk shirt and a black bespoke suit, and from an angle she spotted a pair of long legs, with one leg crossed over the other, with a pair of black Italian bespoke shoes on his feet.

His fingers rested on his brow. His face was handsome and clean-shaven, and Alex's legs wobbled at the sight of him. She glanced past Max to see Crystal waving at her and mouthing, "He's mine."

"What would you like to drink, Mr. Blackstone?"

"Why, Max, do you know this beautiful woman?" St. John asked, leaning forward and softly touching Alex's wrist. "You don't have to answer; I can see it in your face."

"I'm having what Charles is having."

"A glass of water. I'll be right back, Mr. Blackstone." Alex made a quick turn and rushed to Crystal.

"Crystal, Mr. Blackstone wants a glass of water."

"That's all? I'm disappointed. I thought maybe if he had a drink he would make a pass at me." Crystal's head swayed with delight.

"Trust me, you don't want what he's giving."

"I would like to find out. Looking at his face, I can imagine it between my legs and my legs wrapped around that handsome—"

"Okay, Crystal, keep your panties on." Placing a glass on her tray, Crystal walked with poise to the table. She posed standing away from Max, so she could bend forward to show off her breasts. She placed the water glass in front of Max and poured water from the carafe, gazing into his face. His body turned to face Alex, watching her standing at the corner of the bar.

Crystal rushed to Alex. "I think he's gay. I did everything and he never even noticed me. You know how everyone says I have these incredible boobs; well, he never looked twice at them. Mr. St. John couldn't keep his eyes off them, but he's clearly into you."

"Trust me, he's not gay, and no one is into me, Crystal. St. John is just horny. Maybe his wife hasn't given him any in months," Alex said, preparing the garnish for another round of drinks.

Standing at the corner of the bar with her back to the table, she heard, "Alex, I need to speak to you." Max stood behind her, his voice strong and demanding.

"We have nothing to say to each other," Alex said, trying to meet his strength.

"Max." A hand rested on his shoulder. "We don't allow our waitresses to date the clients."

"Does that include you, St. John?" Max's voice rang harsh and confrontational. He never turned around, with his eyes blazing and his brow furrowed.

"Clearly Ms. Bishop does not want to talk to you."

"Is he speaking for you, Alex?" Max questioned with a steely glance.

"Yes."

Max turned on his heel and locked eyes with Charles St. John. "Don't ever come between me and mine. I will forgive it this one time, but not twice. If you value your hotels, then don't cross me, or interfere with me and Alex. We have a history together and you don't understand, and I'm not about to stand here and explain why I'm talking to her."

"Maximilian, you may scare others and that little girl, but you don't scare me, and since you feel the need to threaten me, it is you who need to worry. I will do everything in my power to protect her from you. Please, leave, Max. We have been friends a long time and respect each other, but you are out of order," St. John declared.

"The only thing out of order is for you to come between me and Alex. I will not allow anyone to separate me from Alex. She is mine."

"I've heard you say that before, Max," St. John said.

Alex's eyes widened. *What the fuck does he mean? I am not the only one he has declared that they belonged to him. They appear to have a history of disagreements over women. I wonder who won. I want to be on the side of the winner.*

"Leave, Max," Alex said with strength in her voice. Max's stare remained long after he had gone.

"Are you okay, Alex... Ms. Bishop? Can I see you home?"

"I think I may need a ride," Alex said. She was distraught, thinking that she was fired.

"Ms. Bishop, my limo will take you home." Alex stumbled along and threw a coat on and told Crystal to drive her Volkswagen home after her shift had ended.

Chapter 12

Walking in a daze, I stepped into the limousine as I had done many times with Max; it just appeared to be normal, as normal as the rain falling on my face on a spring day, and as unlucky as drowning in a teaspoon of water.

"Mr. St. John, I wasn't aware that you would accompany me home." I was startled by his presence and seeing him sitting in his limo.

"Please, don't be uneasy. I haven't been able to function since my wife died. I just need the company of a woman."

Why me? I wondered. Clearly he was a man who wouldn't have a problem getting a date. Maybe it was a woman who didn't care for a date that turned him on.

Max had unnerved me to the point that I couldn't drive home without wrecking my car and probably taking out a family in the process. It wasn't me I cared about; it was our son. My fear was that I might die and leave him to Max and Jonas. With Max's obsessive sexual behavior, he would never be around to take care of Maxim, and then there was his post-traumatic-stressed brother, Jonas.

There is no way in hell I will put myself in jeopardy with the possibility of those two having influence over my son.

"Oh, I'm sorry to hear about your loss. I'm not very good company today," I said, focusing on the conversation.

"Don't be sorry. We were high-school sweethearts, and we had more time together than most couples."

How profound. I have been with Max only months, and I may never have the kind of relationship this man enjoyed with his wife. I looked in his face. His black hair had begun to gray on the sides. He was confident, and his clear bluish-gray eyes aroused my body. He might have seen the desires that I harbored, not for him but for Max. *It's probably a hormonal thing.* I looked for the moon. *A full moon,* I thought.

"Where do you know Max from? You don't appear to be the kind of woman he would be interested in."

That statement hit me hard. I sat back and then sat up. "Why would you say that?"

"Because you're not a virgin. Your personal information states that you have a child."

"What else does it say? Does it tell you about my sexual orientation or how I like my men?"

"Please, accept my apology, Ms. Bishop. I didn't mean to—"

I was angry, and I had to let out steam. "I accept your apology, and thank you for the ride home," I said with bitterness in my voice. Max was turning me off men. I didn't know how to be charming. I saw far too much in their faces, which made me defensive. I found myself not trusting them. This should not happen at my age. It wasn't supposed to be like this. I was supposed to find my Prince Charming and marry him, and live happily ever after.

Finally, home. St. John offered to see me to my door. I refused. I stepped out of the limo and staggered into my house to find my roommate, Crystal, watching my thirty-two-inch flat-screen television, which I had purchased at a bargain basement sale. She had a large bowl of popcorn and a can of cola. "What took you so long?" I hadn't noticed that St. John might have taken the scenic route to my home.

"The... the traffic was heavy."

"This time of night?" Crystal raised an eyebrow as if she didn't believe me. "Alex, that gorgeous man, you know the one I had been eyeing most of the night? He stopped me as I was pulling into the driveway." I looked at Crystal, wondering who she could be talking about, because it was well past 2 a.m. "You know, the one I thought was gay. He said he would be back to see you." A loud sound of a fist hitting the door, I knew it was my Mr. Black, and by the sound of the knock, he was angry.

"Crystal, I need some privacy to handle this." Crystal had a look of admiration on her face. It should have been one of concern.

"I wish it was me," Crystal added, wandering into her bedroom and closing the door. I heard music playing, which was great to mask the yelling that was sure to occur.

Opening the door, I placed my hand to my heart as if I could calm the thumping in my chest. His face was intense, his lips inviting, his body hot, and I wanted to jump into his arms, wrap my legs around his waist, and fuck him all night.

"Why would you allow St. John to bring you home?"

"What business is it of yours?"

"Can I come in, Alex, just for a minute?" My gorgeous man walked in and didn't give me a chance to say no, and he sat down. He looked around. "I'm concerned about you. St. John is a man that has peculiar sexual habits."

"Like you, Max. You're worried about what I do in bed. You, who have just about wrecked my life."

"I deserve that. But you don't understand. He's a dangerous man."

"You're a dangerous man."

"I would never do anything to hurt you."

"You already have, so please leave now." Max put his head down and didn't say a word, and placed his hands in his pockets, and lumbered out of the door.

I closed the door and lay with my face and body leaning on the door. I wanted to run to him and fall to my knees and hold on to his fine, muscular legs for dear life, and allow him to fuck me wherever and whenever he wanted. I could feel his dick in my vagina in my dreams. I could feel his body enter mine. All the closeness I craved from being in his presence for however short or long our life together had been, it came back in a torrent of desire.

He has hurt me deeply and we may never find each other.

Waking early the next morning, I made coffee for myself and Crystal. I was a year older than Crystal. Crystal, all of twenty-two and full of my lost youthful arrogance, liked to spend her mornings in bed, except when she smelled a good cup of java. But this morning she was working on her beauty sleep. She was a beauty, but you couldn't tell by the losers she hung out with. Her black hair was now cut short like a boy's, or maybe she'd had extensions, and the red streak was long gone. She wore a size four in dresses, which made me envious of her, because she could eat everything and never gain weight.

After pouring my coffee, a ping registered, and I saw I had an e-mail. When I checked it, I found it was from work.

Ms. Bishop,

I have been informed that you are not working the night shift and that Mr. St. John states that you will accompany him to the opening of his new hotel. He will send you several gowns, and you can select one for the occasion.

Is he out of his fucking mind? I never agreed to—

My thoughts were interrupted by a loud ring from my smartphone.

"Ms. Bishop, this is Charles St. John."

"Yes, Mr. St. John, I recognize your voice."

"I was wondering whether you would join me at the opening of my new hotel."

"I don't know, Mr. St. John."

"Please call me Charles or Charlie, whichever one you prefer."

"Well, Charles, I—"

"As a courtesy to me... my wife... well, I'm not good at being alone."

"Since you put it that way, I will be happy to accompany you this once."

"Thank you, Alex. You won't regret it."

I'm already regretting it. I fell into my chair and had just sipped the last drops of coffee, when at about 10 a.m., a knock on the door jarred me from my seat. I peeped through the small opening on the Shaker door and spotted two women carrying garment bags. I opened the door, and they marched in and hung the dresses on an iron rod. Under the dresses were six pairs of shoes.

Thank God I could walk in high heels, because the Christian Louboutin and Manolo Blahnik heels were five and six inches. *It must be wonderful to be rich and have so much information at your fingertips, but then I have Google, but not the time*, I thought. I thanked the girls and asked them what I should do with the extra dresses, and they said that they were a present from St. John.

I didn't feel comfortable keeping the dresses, and I didn't know when I would be able to use them. As I was going through the dresses looking for something I might wear with a strange man, in walked Crystal, who stopped in her tracks and let out a scream. "Holy shit. Where did you...? Who sent these?"

Crystal's large blue eyes opened wide. She rushed to the dresses and began caressing them as if they were babies. "Look at the labels and the prices."

"Don't get too excited. I'm keeping only one. I'm sending the rest back after tonight."

"But why?" she moaned. The sounds coming from her were like those of a girl who had been told that her first boyfriend had just dumped her on the night of the prom.

"Crystal, I have to go to a function tonight and I need you to work in my place. My customers are big tippers, and you can make pretty good money."

"Okay, but who are you going on a date with?" she murmured in a daze, trying on the shoes.

"I'm going to a function with Mr. St. John."

"Holy shit. You just started working at his hotel and already you have managed to snag two billionaires."

"I didn't snag anything."

"Maybe they have a friend that you could introduce me to, or a wayward brother. Those kinds of guys are always attracted to me."

I thought about Jonas Blackstone. You didn't get more confused and wayward than him. I wasn't going to be responsible for introducing his sick ass to impressionable Crystal. She had just moved to Seattle from Iowa. She didn't need a crazy, unstable man like Jonas messing up her life before she had a chance to live. I wouldn't do that to her. She would have to do that to herself.

Then I thought of Joshua. They looked as if they could make it. After all, he lived on a farm, and Iowa was nothing but farming country.

"Yeah… sure, Crystal," I said, thinking I could keep Joshua out of my hair, but in my life.

Chapter 13

Along with the dresses and numerous silk undergarments was a note telling me when St. John's limousine would pick me up and carry me to the hotel. Crystal had gone to work, and I spent my time trying to fix my unruly hair until a knock came. The woman introduced herself as a stylist. She was sent by St. John. Just in time to save the day. By nine o'clock I had dressed and was waiting for the limo.

When I peered out the window, I saw the limo and out stepped St. John dressed in a traditional black designer tux with white shirt and black bow tie. When he reached the door, I opened it. He had a bouquet of red roses and handed it to me. I felt special again. Then he pulled a black box from his pocket and opened it. The most beautiful teardrop necklace of diamonds and rubies fell into his hands. "It matches your dress."

"How did you know?"

"I didn't know, so I bought one for each dress." His blue-gray eyes didn't lie or appear false, and because of that I found him most attractive. He was indeed appealing with his good looks and easy manner. Not as attractive as Mr. Black, but who was? He had coarse black-and-white hair, and he could have been a ringer for George Clooney at forty.

When Charles smiled, I let down my guard, because his smile was so straightforward and honest. I couldn't imagine that man wanting to tie me up and spank me. His quiet eyes hid a natural quest for excitement and radiated sex appeal. *I guess I'm attracted to quiet men.* I discovered that I was attracted to this quiet storm—this temptation in black.

He walked me to the car, his driver opened the door, and I climbed in. Charles St. John strolled to the other side, slid his quiet, handsome self in, and faced me.

"I hope you don't think that I asked you out because of my grief. I noticed you and you remind me..." He stared long but didn't complete the sentence. "I know it's too soon to say that I am attracted to you, and hope you will consider dating me."

What the fuck? I can't date you or anyone with Black dogging my every move. He's waiting for me to slip up, and then I won't get a chance to get my son back.

"I know you have a son, and I wouldn't do anything to cause you any problems. As a matter of fact, I can probably help you, because I have lawyers on my payroll that specialize in family matters."

"Charles, I don't want to talk about that now. I'm happy that you invited me out and I will have a chance to relax for once."

We arrived at the hotel, and it was more like an opening for a movie. Max's fundraiser was different from many hotel openings. It was filled with older, reserved billionaires.

Charles's hotel had young and exciting people from different backgrounds who came to drink, dance, and get laid. *Where does St. John fit in?* I questioned. We stepped out of the limo, and cameras were flashing all around, and I was blinded by them. Charles grabbed my arm and looped it under his and led me through the doors and into the entrance of this magnificent palace with chandeliers hanging from the ceiling every few yards. Someone pulled St. John in the direction of a group of men and asked that he introduce me.

"Is she your daughter?"

Charles smiled and said, "Good Lord, man, I'm only thirty-five."

"It must be the hair." And then I heard whispers ringing like the peal of a bell. "Blackstone... Blackstone... Blackstone."

I turned to see Max sauntering in with Ms. Corday. I guessed they were an item now. The smile on her face signaled that she had been fucked within an inch of her life. She clung to his arm as if he was the last man on earth, and he was my last man on earth.

Glancing at Corday, I spotted her leaning in and whispering in Max's ear. His eyes shifted my way; he pulled his arm from hers and strode in my direction. St. John had been corralled by a group of women dying for his attention. I found the nearest bar and ordered wine, and then I heard, "What are you doing here, and with St. John?"

I turned and looked into his incredibly handsome face. I could feel the intense longing for whatever he could give me, and that was just at a glance with his devilish green eyes.

"You have no right to ask me anything."

"Is he bothering you, Alex?" St. John asked. I turned to see Charles standing close behind me with a drink in his hand.

"He's calling you Alex now?" Max's voiced lowered a few octaves.

"This is my hotel, Blackstone, and this is my party, and she is my guest. I did not invite you. Do I have to have you removed?"

"Don't worry. I'm leaving." Max left wearing a sinister expression, his brow furrowed. I had never seen his face truly angry. A chill crossed my spine and left me cold. The warmth of St. John's arm gave me comfort.

"Don't worry, Alex. He can't hurt you, not with me around."

"Max would never try to hurt me intentionally."

"But he has, hasn't he? You two have a son together and he bribed a judge to give him custody. From my investigation, he and the judge were roommates in college. That is something that is not common knowledge, especially for the type of lawyer who represented you."

"It was all I could afford," I murmured, angry to find out the truth about Max's underhanded dealings.

"The cards were stacked against you. Even if you brought in an expensive lawyer who would cost you hundreds of thousands of dollars, it would not be enough for a billionaire who has connections and who knows everyone's secrets. There is only one man in this town that can handle Maximilian."

"Whoever he is, I can't afford him."

"You are standing here with him, and he finds you ravishing." I looked at Charles St. John and saw him for the first time. He was as handsome as Max. He began to appeal to me in a way that Max had not. Because I was so in love with Max, I couldn't stand to look at another man. Because Max had introduced me to his sexual lifestyle, I had forgotten that there were men who were like I used to be—vanilla. Because I was afraid of Max, I ran from him to make a life for myself. I had been running in ever decreasing circles.

There was no place to run far enough where he could not find me and my son. So now I had to take a stand and fight him, and Charles could be my ammunition and my shield.

"Alex, I don't have children because my wife died early, and she had trouble conceiving. I understand how empty she felt, and I don't want you to go through that. I will do everything I can to get your son back."

"I need a job, and not in a hotel as a cocktail waitress. Can you help me? Max owns most of the companies in Seattle, and he sent out a memo that I was not to be hired by any firm, hotel, bank, or newspaper."

"I never received that memo. I own several banks, and if you're serious, then I can hire you tomorrow." I leaned over and kissed Charles on the cheek with enthusiasm of a teenage girl receiving a corsage for the prom. His face lit up, and the pain of loss was erased from his brow.

"Let's have a glass of champagne," St. John stated eagerly.

"I thought you didn't drink."

"That's only at meetings. I like to keep a clear head and watch my staff. I need to know who throws down more liquor than they should. In my business, you have to know everything that's going on. I have airline contracts, and my managers have to be levelheaded, or else people will die. Take Max—that man never misses a meeting, night or day, and whatever country his business takes him to, he is there and stone-cold sober. I admire him. I don't know how he does it. I guess that will end now that he has a son to care for."

I know how he does it. He gets in a big dose of fucking and then marches off without a care in the world. That was until I left him, and he found out he had a child. I bet his business is suffering now.

A business partner took St. John from our table, so I headed for the nearest restroom. I hadn't made it to the door when I felt a hand on my shoulder. It was a light touch, but a firm one. I knew it was not Max, because his touch caused my body to quake whenever he placed his hand on me. I turned around to see Blake Scotto dressed in a dark suit and white shirt with an earpiece dangling from his ear.

"What are you doing here, Blake?"

"I'm working. Some of us have to work for a living to pay for a meal out once a month." He gave a light smile. His best assets were his teeth and his smile. I thought he should smile more; that smile could stop a woman in her tracks. "I would ask you the same thing if I didn't know that you were hanging with the billionaire club."

"I wouldn't exactly say hanging with billionaires. You don't hang with them. I couldn't keep up with them if I wanted to, and I don't want to."

"I saw you earlier and I wanted to speak to you. I want to tell you how amazing you look. Expensive jewels do nothing for you." Blake's fingers caressed my necklace, and my eyes followed his fingers. I looked around to see if St. John had seen Blake. St. John's back was turned. It might prove awkward explaining to Charles that I knew his security officer. Not that I cared to make the explanation, but I just wasn't in the mood to answer questions.

"You were more beautiful without all those garish diamonds. But if I had diamonds to give you, I would probably shower them on you too."

"I explained to you that I'm not that kind of girl. I was thrust into this world, and I can't seem to escape."

"If you ever get out, call me. You do have my card?" I shook my head yes. He put his hand to his ear. "I'm being contacted. I think my boss is worried about our conversation. We're not supposed to fraternize with the guests, especially a special personal guest of Mr. St. John."

"It was great seeing you, Blake." At that moment I wanted to be B.B. Before Blackstone. I wanted to be twenty-one in my own little apartment in Brooklyn, dating casually, no problems but one, and it sure wasn't men.

Now I was miserable. Maybe that was what happened when you fell in love young—you were perpetually miserable when you couldn't be with the one you loved, and didn't want to love the one you were with!

———— ◉ ————

I DRANK EXPENSIVE CHAMPAGNE all night with Charles to celebrate our newly formed partnership. Charles and I got drunk, and when I entered his limo for my ride home, one of my expensive shoes fell somewhere under the seat. Arriving at my door, I stepped out of the car and looked down. I couldn't walk. Charles swept me up in his arms. I looked at him with a drunken gaze; I wanted it to be Max. I held him around his neck with both hands and placed my cheek close to his, and we both felt the yearning. We were two eager souls drifting in each other's direction, ready for a collision.

Standing on the porch of my bungalow, the light provided a spotlight aimed at our faces. Not that anything would occur, but I didn't want Max to make something out of nothing to use against me.

Crystal had turned on the light early in case I made it home late. I fidgeted around in my small evening bag that could only hold a pack of cigarettes. And since I didn't smoke, I found a small comb, a lipstick, and finally my keys.

I had left my phone at home, charging in the docking station, and when I opened the door, I heard it ringing on the dining-room table. There was no way I would answer it, because it was Max. I chose to ignore it and concentrate on the very handsome, very sane, and very tempting Charles St. John.

Charles held me in his arms. My glance fell to the floor, and I motioned with my head, and he deposited me with ease before kissing my cheek and pulling down my long dress that had somehow tightened and wrapped around my thighs. *What a wonderful gesture*, I thought.

"I had a great time." I was trying to be polite without trying to be obligated.

"Maybe you would consider another date with me?"

What the fuck can I say? Yes, I want to date you, because I'm starved for attention from a man. Yes, I want to date you, because you may be the only man that can prevent Max from keeping my son. "Maybe. But for now, I have to get up early tomorrow and prepare for a new job. As well as having a roommate that will probably be in here asking about my date with you. She has a crush on you." I smiled, hoping he would let me off the hook and take up with Crystal instead.

"You don't have to go to work tomorrow. Just rest and prepare to work at my bank. I will have my secretary e-mail you some paperwork that will explain your duties. I should have everything arranged, and by next week you can start."

"I don't want—"

He placed his finger to my mouth to silence me. And then he placed his lips over his finger and then removed both. I felt young again. I was being wooed and not expected to receive a body in the middle of the night telling me that he needed my body parts, as if I could package them one at a time and send them to him. I hadn't missed that about Max. I just missed Max.

Charles left and closed the door behind him. I watched through the picture window and saw his limo pull away. I stood in the middle of the floor, dancing and breathing, not knowing which way to turn. I knew I had to lock the door.

Reaching for the lock, I heard a knock, and in strutted Max. There he stood in a black suit and white shirt. He'd obviously had time to change. Maybe he'd gotten in a fuck with Ms. Corday before coming for a second round. I gazed down at his well-shined black shoes. No loafers. This was not a casual call. In his hand he held a paper. "Did you see the *New York Post*?" he asked, waving it in front of him.

"I never buy the *Post*. It's nothing but a glorified rag."

"In the *Post* there are pictures of you and St. John. The question on the front page is, 'Who is that woman at his side? Are we seeing the next Mrs. St. John?'" he said, reading the paper and then looking up at me. "Very soon the world will know who you are, and you and our son will not be safe."

Now it was clear why Max didn't invite me to his functions. He was trying to protect me.

"That may explain one thing, but it does not explain why you would take Corday to the opening of Charles's hotel."

"You're taking to referring to him as Charles." Max bristled. "The person you saw was not me, Alex." It became clear about Corday, but it took a little time before I knew the answer.

"Who was it?" I wanted him to answer this question, then I wouldn't have to make wrong assumptions and drive myself crazy.

"The person you saw was Jonas." His eyes lowered. "I have businesses all over the world and sometimes I can't make all of my meetings. I can't allow my competitors to see my weakness. St. John is one and now he knows that you are mine and he will do anything to get you. He's not what you think he is."

"And neither are you, and don't refer to me as yours, as if I'm one of your possessions."

"I deserved that, Alex. You don't know how vicious he can be." He moved closer, and the electricity that existed between us had grown.

Not seeing him and wanting him had heightened my sexual senses. His face excited me, his eyes stunned me, and I could not and would not move from that spot. His smell aroused my basest of instincts, and I waited for him to take me and do whatever he wanted—tie me up, fuck me and then whip my ass—you name it, he was welcome to do it all. I was open to anything at that moment. It had been too long since he had put his mouth on my clit, and it had been too long since I had experienced an orgasm.

Holding on to my senses, I said, "What can be more vicious than taking a child from his mother?"

Max's head fell low. He felt my hurt. He raised his head and placed his hands to my face. "Not telling a father that he has a son." I froze. "Can we go to your room?" His voice was soft. I didn't expect that. I wasn't used to that. I didn't want that. I wanted my take-charge man again. Not begging to take me to my room, but dragging me as he tore my clothes off along the way. I wanted to go scratching and clawing his back in full resistance. But I went shamelessly quiet, and he remained the gentleman I thought I wanted and that he tried to become.

I grabbed his hand and led him to my little room with my white sheets and white comforter, on a white wrought-iron bed with a wrought-iron headboard. I turned on my old, white-painted lamp with the new lampshade. He placed his smartphone on the distressed white table under my painted lamp. He dropped his house keys and a black silk ribbon and his prep school tie all on that table. And we sat facing each other on the edge of the bed.

He looked around. "This is me," I said. "Not that palace I lived in, which you owned."

"What do you want me to do, Alex?"

"I want my son back, and I want to get a job that you can't take from me."

"I can't give back my wealth; it's me, just as much as my face, or Jonas. I'm stuck with this." He paused, searching my eyes, and hoping

I would understand. "You shouldn't work at places where you can be kidnapped and held for ransom. Why do you think I took my son? Once my enemies discover that they can get to me through my son and you, I could lose everything that I care about." I recognized the truth when I heard it. Now I realized that he was concerned about our son's safety and my well-being.

"I will give you back our son against my better judgment and leave you alone to work out your life. But you will have to accept a bodyguard. I know you are young, and things have been happening fast—"

"Oh, Max, just give me a little time and you will be so proud of me, then we will take it from there." As usual I had selective hearing. I didn't hear about the bodyguard until it was too late. I agreed to what Max wanted and blanked out the rest. I had this thing about not hearing something and not reading the small print, which had come back to bite me in the ass, literally.

"I have another stipulation."

"What?"

"I want the opportunity to introduce you to a higher level of reaching an orgasm."

That sounded great to me. I didn't think that there was anything that I hadn't done with Max. My Max was back and in full force.

He gazed at me with a strange look, eyes dark and brow furrowed, and then he reached for my ruby-red evening gown, and with both hands, pulled it, tearing the expensive silk gown until the slit reached under my breasts. "You didn't accept my clothes, so you will never wear St. John's dress again."

I hadn't planned on ever wearing it again, but my clit heated up to its boiling point when I understood how jealous he was when he thought there was another man snooping around. He had marked his territory like the Alpha male that he was.

Pulling my panties down, I stepped out of them. He sniffed the crotch before discarding them in the corner, and then he inserted his finger into my vagina and looped it around. Pulling it out, he placed it to his nose. "You're tight and moist. I can tell that St. John didn't get to first base. Tell me you're mine."

"I'm yours."

"You will never belong to another man."

Maybe there is something in the contract that I signed when I agreed to be Max's sub that I didn't read. Perhaps I should take a look at it. Give it a once-over to be sure I didn't miss something that may have long-term consequences to me. After all, I'm only twenty-three; whose knows what may happen in the future.

He put his head between my legs, and his tongue found my clit. He rose up and said, "Your bud is eager." Just when I was enjoying every minute of his salacious lovemaking, he reached for something and said, "Here. Tie this ribbon around your eyes."

"What?"

"Do it. You have to trust me, Alex. That is part of our life together. I tried being another person. I tried seeing you as a mother and not my partner, and that didn't work. We are sexual human beings. We are drawn to each other, because of our attraction and the way we connect during sex."

I tried to analyze what Max said in those few moments. It made sense. I could recognize when I heard the truth, and the truth was that we were attracted to each other whether we were parents or not. When we were in bed, nothing mattered but the love and the loving we gave each other.

I tied the black ribbon around my eyes, and I felt completely vulnerable. I trusted him. I was eager to please him. I still thought of the woman who was strangled in his hotel, but when he placed his face back in a familiar position—between my legs—I forgot about anything but having him make love to me.

Not seeing anything connected me to my body in the most erotic way. All my senses came alive, and I felt each flick of his tongue as he licked my folds and the creases between my legs and mound. His tongue moved slowly as he inched me toward an orgasm. He paused a moment to say, "I love sucking your clit. I can feel it vibrate in my mouth, and it makes me harder."

I can't imagine his dick being any harder than it is. My leg eased along his rod, and it felt hotter than any time before.

I wrapped my legs around his body and begged, "Can I come?"

"Now you are being my submissive." I could feel through the blindfold that he had a smile on that gorgeous face when he planted his head between my legs. I had given in to him in bed. It was what I needed, and it was all that Max desired—to have his way with me in bed.

He flicked his tongue on my clit, and damn, I had an orgasm that made my scalp tremble and my body shake. I reached to untie the ribbon. "No, you will keep it on until we are finished and because you have been naughty and decided to date another man, I'm going to paddle you with my hand, and then I'll decide what to do next."

"But—"

"But nothing, Alex." Max took my hands and placed them behind my back. "Now I want you to suck me without touching me with your hands. Only your mouth." He pulled me up and propped my back against the iron bed and straddled me. "Take it and put it in your mouth." I felt for it with my mouth, and it was directly in front of me, extending like a cobra ready to strike. Leaning into my mouth, Max guided it in, hitting my lips along the way. I took it in and glided my tongue around and over his slit. He leaned over me, thrusting in and out. I felt the perspiration trickle from his chest. His smell was intoxicating. The more sweat poured into my face the more I became excited. I felt the telltale signs of his orgasm. He was on the edge of coming, and I wanted to push him over into the abyss as he had done to me.

"I'm there, Alex. I want this now." I slowed my movements with my mouth, and I reached around him for his hard buttocks. I felt them stiffen, and I dug my false nails into them, and he flinched from the pain. "Don't hold back. I need to come now."

Don't tell me when and how you need to come. You are not in control, my handsome fuck. If you are in such control of your body then you don't need to beg me for your orgasm, I thought.

I began to work my mouth, sucking in and out, demonstrating to him what I was capable of doing. I sucked him hard, and he spilled his hot come in my mouth. It kept coming until it flowed like a river down the sides of my chin, and he still kept fucking my mouth.

"I can't stop. I'm having another one," he confessed. The feral grunts and moans were akin to a wounded animal, and I knew that a wounded animal was dangerous. "How are you capable of doing this to me?" Max paused to take a breath and remove his dick from my mouth. He fell to the side of me, panting. "You are a dangerous girl, Alex. I have to keep an eye on you." I smiled a devilish smile, and he knew that he had created a monster.

"I don't like that smile."

"What are you going to do about it?" In that second he turned me over and began smacking my butt.

"Stop it, Max. I was just kidding," I said, laughing.

"I'm not." I felt his dick rise when he leaned close to smack my butt, then he stopped, and one hand moved to my clit and the other gripped my ass. He circled my ass with his tongue, making it moist, and then he forced his wonderful face between my ass cheeks. I could hear and feel his breath, and then I felt that glorious tongue, by now my best friend in the world, a friend I could depend on to satisfy me sexually and make me happy when I was sad, a friend that would be there rain or shine when I was lonely, and a friend that would never let me down.

My friend pulled away from me, and his friend thrust his dick into my vagina and filled my walls with his penis. "I can't seem to get enough of you. What's going to become of me, Alex?" he said, fucking me in and out and fucking some more. He placed his hand to buttress my stomach from the onslaught of his hard, needy dick that was plundering every part of my body. The dark scarf had blinded me, and my senses were acute. I felt every blow his long, hard dick inflicted on me, and through the pain and pleasure, I had my third orgasm of the night. His breathing was erratic and his dick still hard. He was not done with me.

"I said that I would introduce you to something perverse in lovemaking, but I don't know whether you are ready yet."

"What is it, Max?"

"You will have to wait until we are married to find out, because you are not ready, and your room is not conducive for this. We need silence and freedom from anyone knowing what we are doing. I bet your roommate has a glass to the wall. I have a house just fit for that. It is being built for us at this time."

Max just said that he would give me time, and now he is building houses without consulting me. I don't know about this. And did I forget about Charles through the incredible lovemaking Max just laid on me? What am I doing? I don't know how to tell Max that I have a job at one of St. John's banks. Well, he never discloses anything to me. I guess this will have to be on a need-to-know basis, and he doesn't need to know, at least not now, just when I got my Mr. Black back.

Chapter 13

We were awakened by the chime coming from Max's phone. The sun was up, and it had to be about 7 a.m. I wasn't going to work. I pushed Max, and he turned over.

"Max. Max, your phone." Max reached for the phone.

"Who is it?" His eyes widened.

"No. Oh no. Not him. I thought it would be me." He sat up in the bed, shirtless, resting on the headboard. Tears streamed from his eyes. "I'm coming now. Call the local police and then contact the FBI."

"What is it, Max? What is it?"

"Don't worry. I have it under control."

"What do you have under control? You haven't told me anything."

"Sit up."

"Why?"

"Just do what I say for once, Alex."

"I'm sitting up. Now tell me."

There was a long pause, and his eyes closed and opened. "Our son has been... kidnapped."

I didn't hear him. My selective hearing took over, because all I heard was "our son."

Max's voice wavered and died out, and the background noise from the street took over. It wasn't the background noise; there wasn't any noise. It was the sounds in my head screaming at me. And I began to scream.

"Alex, stop. I'll handle it. Trust me."

"You were the one that took my son. You were the one that promised he would be safe."

"Calm down, honey. Calm down. No one would dare hurt my son. I have resources to track them down. But first I have to notify the authorities, and I have to get my security detail involved, and before I can do that I will need you to calm down and listen to me."

"I'm calm now."

"I'm going in the other room to contact everyone I know that can help me. Okay?"

"Okay," I said, trembling.

He stayed in the living room for an hour. By that time, I had showered and had my bag packed. He came in to say that we were going to Montana. That was where he'd had Maxim, and that was where Maxim had disappeared. He moved about with slow, deliberate steps, looking as if he had just spent time climbing a mountain, and it had conquered him.

"My limo is waiting outside. I'll take a shower on our flight. We should be there in an hour with the ride to the airport and all."

I reached for my bag, and Max took it from my hands. He held it as he walked ahead of me, opening the door. "Wait. I have to leave a note for Crystal."

"No. Text her," Max said in his take-charge voice. "The time is important." And he placed his hand behind my back and ushered me into the limo. Max was silent traveling to the airfield. He appeared to be mapping something out in his mind, something that he did not want to include me in. "I need to call Jonas. He should be informed. He was in Special Forces, and he will be instrumental in the search."

Max took the phone that rested in his limo and tried calling, but I could tell from his expression that he wasn't having any luck. "God damn it. He is never around when you need him." He tried over and over until we landed in Billings, Montana. I looked around, and it was surreal, as if I had never left. I felt the wind and the smell of fresh air and the bristle of the dry climate. When we entered the limo, he tried calling again. After not reaching Jonas, Max decided to leave a message.

We rounded a bend in the road and stopped at Max's mountain retreat. It was as I remembered, beautiful and secluded. Max jumped out, extending his hand, and helping me out. As we walked into the house, he said, "I thought that when I brought you home to Montana, I would be bringing you as my bride." He held my luggage with one hand, and the other was on the small of my back.

The first time I saw this place, I was twenty, impressionable, and in Max's arms. Now I was twenty-three and I'd seen too much, and it was not a very good year.

"Welcome back, Mr. Blackstone, Mrs. Blackstone." The servants greeted us as a married couple. "I don't know what happened. One minute Maxim was playing on the grounds next to the swings, and the next minute he was gone," the nanny explained with tears in her eyes.

"I don't have time to talk, Pilar. Get Alex... Mrs. Blackstone's bags. Would you like something to drink, Alex?"

"I don't want anything. I need a clear head."

"Then show Mrs. Blackstone to our room."

"I would rather—" He interrupted my conversation and thoughts with his take-charge, do-it-my-way self.

"Look, Alex, I have this under control."

"The way I see it you have nothing under control. Maxim is missing..."

"Do you want to fight and let the servants see?"

"I don't give a damn what they see."

"Go to our room."

"Now you are sending me to the room as if I'm a child. Which room am I to go to? The one where you—" I didn't want to finish that thought. "Or the one that no woman is allowed into?"

"The one no woman but you has seen. I'll join you shortly. Remember, I'm trying to get our son back, and you're not making anything any easier. The men I requested for the search are on their way now, and I can't find Jonas."

I left Max talking on the phone. I hadn't been back since I marched out of that door and swore I would never return, and that was three years ago. I staggered past the room where Max had taken my virginity. Feeling weak from worry, my guilt about Maxim lifted when I saw the bed, and it made me smile because even though I was angry it had to have been the most exciting moment in my life. I peeped in just to relive that moment when Max sat across from me and asked me to feel his heart.

From a simple gesture and a complicated relationship with Max, our baby was born. I took a great sigh and moved on into the room where I had been for only a moment. I looked around and walked to his medicine cabinet, looking for something stronger than aspirin to calm my nerves. My hands touched a bottle of Excedrin PM. "This will do the trick. I want to be dead to the world. Maybe by the time I wake up Max will have located Maxim, or the kidnappers will have been caught."

I swallowed two tablets, and I looked around and picked up some bottled water from the counter and drank it. I took off my clothes found one of Max's shirts and sat on the bed. I spied a figure of a man standing in the doorway. It was Max's butler. "Is everything okay, Mrs. Blackstone?" I didn't know why everyone on Max's staff kept referring to me as Mrs. Blackstone, but I would take it up with him later.

"I'm fine."

"Can I get you anything to eat?"

"I'm not hungry."

"Then I'll let you sleep."

⸺⸺●⸺⸺

I WOKE WITH MAX STARING down at me. "Are you okay?"

"What time is it? And how long have I been sleeping?"

"It's about 6 a.m. I thought it better to let you sleep."

"Let me be the judge of that."

"I have everyone looking for our son. I haven't received a note or call for ransom. I had a team of men in the house when you were asleep. A friend of yours is working for me. He came highly recommended by the San Francisco police department." I looked on curiously, expecting Max to tell me sooner or later.

I got tired of waiting and asked, "Who is it?"

"Detective Blake Scotto."

"Why... what possessed you to get him mixed up in our lives?" I said, concerned for Max's safety and Blake's.

"You do want the best. Well, he is best at getting to the truth. And you always keep your enemies close," Max said with dark eyes and a wandering glance.

"How is he an enemy?" My words brought back Max's glance, and it settled on me.

"He wants you." Max undressed, walked into the shower, and closed the door. When he returned he had a restless look about him and a towel covered his hips. He paced the room like a wounded animal. "Damn, Alex, I can't find Jonas. I don't need to worry about my son *and* my brother." He plopped on the bed with the phone to his ear and the towel opened at the center, exposing his body. I went to my knees holding on to his thighs and gazing into his eyes. He needed release from the tension of staying up all night. I took his penis in my hand and placed it in my mouth. I heard him say, "Jonas, call me. Fuck everything else. I need you, brother." It was clear that he needed me more than I needed him. He dropped the phone, and his head swung back with his mouth open wide. He raked his fingers through my hair as he held my head, whispering, "I don't know what I would do without you and my son. You two are my life. If I don't have you two, I don't want to live."

Max fell into a deep sleep. I moved away from him and watched as he curled up in a fetal position, like a baby. He stayed in that position facing the enormous floor-to-ceiling window circling the bed. I woke with my arms draped across his waist and my head lying on his shoulder. Max had been sleeping hard, because he didn't feel me remove my arm, scoot across the bed, grab a housecoat and slippers, leave, and close the door behind me.

I smelled coffee and wanted a cup. I headed in the direction of the aroma and found the kitchen. "Good morning."

"Oh, good morning, Mrs. Blackstone," said Rodger Van Horn, Max's butler. "You should have remained in bed, and I would have brought you coffee and breakfast."

Turning to meet my glance, Blake rose from a stool with a cup in his hand, and next to him lay a folder on the counter. We stared silently at each other, waiting for the other to speak. The butler noticed the uncomfortable moment we shared, and walked from the kitchen.

The silence was broken. "What brings you here so early, Mr. Scotto? I hope you have some news about my son. I'm tired from worry."

"I'm sorry, but you don't look any worse for it."

"Mr. Scotto..."

"Please, don't be so formal. I've asked you to call me Blake, remember?" Our eyes met. My lashes lowered. "As a matter of fact, I have some great news." My eyes raised, and my heartbeat quickened. "I've viewed the security cameras, and your son wasn't kidnapped after all. Mr. Blackstone was the last person to see him yesterday."

"That's impossible. Max was in Seattle with me," I said, my voice hoarse, my mind confused and wandering.

"Well, Alex... unless he has a twin, then he is the only one who could have taken his son." My heart screamed with the irony and truth of what Blake had said. I knew little of Jonas Blackstone, only that he was a drop-dead gorgeous man, an identical twin with mental issues.

The End

Book 3 of the Blackstone Series available; book 1 (*The Incredible Mr. Black*) 2, 3 through 9 available where e-books are sold.

Blog: http://www.rachel-e-rice.com

Books by Rachel E. Rice

Blackstone Series Erotic Dark Romance

1. The Incredible Mr. Black
2. Temptation in Black
3. Submission to Black
4. Black Tie Affair
5. Mourning Becomes Black
6. Fade to Black
7. Back to Black
8. Black Tide
9. Black Swan
10. Blackout

Don't miss out!

Visit the website below and you can sign up to receive emails whenever Rachel E Rice publishes a new book. There's no charge and no obligation.

https://books2read.com/r/B-A-ASU-FIZC

BOOKS2READ

Connecting independent readers to independent writers.

Did you love *Temptation In Black*? Then you should read *One Desire*[1] by Rachel E Rice!

When Tyler Burns graduates from a prep school in New Jersey and is the valedictorian of her prestigious high school, she assumes that her working-class background will take her only so far. And it probably would have gotten her a working-class stiff like her father, but she gets more than she expects when she meets Brandon Charles, a Princeton graduate, hot as the noon-day sun, with his blue-green eyes, sexy good looks, and a body to bring her to her knees. It's no wonder he's engaged, and he's expected to marry within a week.

Tyler accepts a ride home with Brandon from the frat party, never intending to end up in his bed at his estate, but she does. And if things can't get worse it does. She stays with him for a week, and most of the

---

1. https://books2read.com/u/m2RNRm

2. https://books2read.com/u/m2RNRm

week is spent in bed. He promises her he will return once he calls off the wedding. And she believes him and waits for him, but he never returns that night, or the next, or the next.

Five years later, she has graduated from college, when Brandon strolls back into her life in a restaurant with a beautiful girl, and Tyler is their waitress.

Read more at www.rachel-e-rice.com.

Also by Rachel E Rice

Blackstone
The Incredible Mr. Black
Blackstone Complete 10 Books Dark Romance Series
Temptation In Black
Blackstone Series 4 Books Box Set
Submission To Black
Black Tie Affair
The Incredible Mr. Black Box Set
Mourning Becomes Black
Fade To Black
Back to Black
Black Tide
Black Swan
Blackout
Blackstone Series 6 Books Box Set

I Am The Night
I Am The Night

Insatiable

Insatiable: The Lone Werewolf finds his mate
Insatiable: A Werewolf's Hunger
Insatiable: A Werewolf's Wedding
Insatiable: The Werewolves' Challenge
Hunter's Moon
Moon Tide
Moon Rapture

Insatiable Werewolf Series
A Bride For A Werewolf: The Beginning
Thorn in Moonscape
Insatiable: Damon in Moonscape
A Werewolf's Passion
Moonscape Box Set

Night
I Am First Night
I Am Last Night

Obsession
Obsession: Warm Bodies,Cold Hearts
Naked Obsession
Burning Obsession

Seduction
Seduced By An Earl

The Captain
The Captain and The Virgin

The Soul of A Vampire
Soul of A Vampire
Soul of A Vampire Book 2
Soul of A Vampire Book 3

To kill a vampire
To Kill a Vampire
To Kill A Vampire
To Kill A Vampire

Standalone
Finding Summer
One Desire
Insatiable Box Set: Books 1-4
Hunter's Moon Box Set
Hunter's Moon Insatiable Series
Insatiable: Tracker #8
Soul of A Vampire Box Set
The Complete Insatiable Werewolf Bundle
The Complete Insatiable Werewolf Bundle
I Am The Night Box Set
A Vampire Bundle
A Vampire Bundle

I Am The Night Box Set
To Kill A Vampire Boxset
To kill A Vampire Boxset
A Complete Vampire Bundle

Watch for more at www.rachel-e-rice.com.

About the Author

Rachel E. Rice enjoys writing in different genres. As an Indie author she explores genres to find her voice. She has written contemporary romance, erotic romance, new adult, historical and science fiction.

When she's not writing she is reading poetry. She has a BA and is a member of Romance Writers of America.

Read more at www.rachel-e-rice.com.

About the Publisher

Rachel E Rice is a member of Romance Writers of America. She writes in different genres. Her readers can find her books under historical, contemporary, paranormal, and erotica romance. When she is not writing, she is reading books in different genres.

"Passion is a great love story."

* 9 7 9 8 2 2 4 6 8 4 2 8 1 *